Audio Distortion

Replay

Available in print and digital formats online at amazon.com

Copyright © 2013 – C Clef Publishing

All rights reserved. No part of this publication may be reproduced, stored in a retrieval system, or transmitted, in any form or by any means, electronic, mechanical, photocopying, recording, or otherwise, without prior written permission from the author.

This is fictional work, and all names, characters, and incidents depicted herein, are real only in the author's imagination. Any similarities to persons living or dead, or events past or present, are pure coincidence.

Book Design: Mike Fontenot

Cover Design: Mike Fontenot

Front Cover Image: Alexander Karnes (http://steamby51.deviantart.com)

Printing History:

Original – July 2013

First Revision – August 2016

Hardcover – October 2015

PRINTED IN THE UNITED STATES OF AMERICA

ISBN-13: 978-1484898611

ISBN-10: 1484898613

10 9 8 7 6 5 4 3 2 1

"Hey Little Miss Nerves, you like to sing that silly pop crap, so why don't you belt one out for these people…"

~Matt Duncan

Prologue

Emily Tao

What is that smell? More importantly, why do I smell it? Oh yeah... the windows are down... I remember. Wait... why are my eyes closed? My eyes are closed? What the...

The moment my eyes open and focus, I panic. I'm not in my Jeep. This can't be. I was driving up US 395 – going home. Willie called... and Stan. We talked... about the show...

I force my eyes to blink... once, twice.

Oh crap... I'm in a hospital room. What the...?

At least that explains the smell.

I'd been thinking about Emma... that's right... her voice coming out of the Jeep's speakers. She's singing... *'Friendship now, Friendship always ...'*

I blink my eyes again. They seem to be working okay. Fingers. I wiggle each of them. They all seem to be there. I do the same with my toes, with the same result. The moment I try to move, I hear a voice to my left – it says my name. As I turn my head that direction – with much effort I should add – I see her, standing there with a pony-tail and a huge frown.

"Emma? What the..."

Now... in order to explain to you why finding Emma Greene standing next to my bed in a hospital, totally freaked me out, we'll have to go back a day – to yesterday morning, in Los Angeles...

one

the interview

"Welcome to VH1 Talks. I'm Donna Dollar – your host.

"Nineteen months ago, I had the privilege of doing the first full on-air interview with what many thought would be the next first family of pop music. The day before the interview, *Audio Distortion's* debut album went multi-platinum a second time, breaking the three million mark, and their digitally released singles *Being Noticed* and *Crazy Road* were both multi-platinum, each having been downloaded well over two million times.

"Since then, as the world knows, in addition to selling out every show they performed, and rocking countries around the world, the members of *Audio Distortion*, suffered a number of frustrating and, in some cases heartrending, complications and setbacks in their lives as musicians, which inevitably led to their breakup last year."

A voice is heard out of the camera's view, and the camera operator quickly adjusts the shot to include a young woman sitting across from Donna.

"Uh... excuse me, Donna, but can I interrupt for just one second?"

"Of course."

"For the record, *Audio Distortion* didn't 'breakup'. That was all 'media fabrication' – no offense intended.

The term 'breakup' is way too negative, and doesn't give a true account of what really happened. Generally speaking, when people 'breakup', it isn't pleasant or friendly. For the record, *Audio Distortion* 'disbanded' – by mutual agreement. I apologize for butting in..."

"Music fans, meet Emily Táo, original lead guitarist for, and founder of, *Audio Distortion*. That isn't the introduction I envisioned, but it works. Emily graciously agreed to come and spend an hour talking with me about the band's meteoric rise to stardom, and their ensuing collapse, as they were individually bombarded with one personal disaster after another, during what would have been their five month maiden tour."

Donna turns away from the camera, and faces Emily.

"Welcome, Emily, and thank you for being willing to share your story with our viewers."

"Thanks for giving me – or *us* actually – the chance to tell the world our story. I have been in contact with everyone in the band – well, almost everyone – and they agree that the *real story* needs to be told. Over the last year and a half, there has been a lot of supposition generated about the members of the band, and in most cases, the press and the tabloids got it wrong. I'm here to answer your questions honestly, and to tell our fans what *really* happened to *Audio Distortion*...."

two

the beginning

Emma Greene

So... as Emily sets about baring our souls for the public, I'm here, in my living room, watching. My name is Emma Greene, and I'm a singer.

As you are about to learn, I'm the big reason we – *Audio Distortion* – are here.

But, in order to understand how we got *here*, it seems you need to know where we *came from*...

Who... and what... is *Audio Distortion*?

It all started my junior year...

*****

Fort Collins, Colorado – an interesting place to grow up. Truth is, I've never been anywhere else.

Well... that's not entirely true. I was actually born in Texas. I came to live with my grandmother, in Colorado when I was five.

Long story – which you will eventually hear.

Anyhow, this is my life.

I go to Ridgeline, which is a 'charter' school that specializes in academics. We don't even have sports teams. But that's cool with me. You see, my passion is language, and our classical literature program is one of the best in the country.

As far back as I can remember, I've always written. Dreams, poems, songs, even stories. The only thing I'd rather do than write – is read. Lately, I've been on a 'classics' kick. I often find myself lost in images of what life would have been like in Shakespeare's day.

I've always been a 'keep to myself' kinda girl, and while I 'know' lots of kids, I have just one real friend. His name is Stanley.

Stanley goes to FCHS – Fort Collins High School. His family lives on a ranch, out near the reservoir, east of the interstate. We met the first time, in the public library, when he came around a corner and, completely by accident, knocked me down. It was actually pretty comical. He kept apologizing as he gathered up the papers and books I was carrying, and the moment our eyes met... well... let's just say I still haven't gotten over it.

About a month later, Stanley texted me, and asked if I might be interested in a job. Once I talked to Grams about it, I texted him back and said I'd give it a try. He called seconds after I sent the text, and told me where to meet him.

It turned out to be a pizzeria about three miles from my house. Until I walked in and saw Stan behind the counter, I had no idea he worked there – for over two years it turns out. When his boss decided to hire extra summer help, Stanley convinced him to give me a chance...

"Emma... are you sure you want to try this? Some of my customers are... well... I mean, this is a college town..."

Mr. Lou Santoro – owner of Papa Roni's – almost seems to be trying to talk me out of the job, mostly because my lack of social skills is blatantly obvious.

"Ahhh... she'll be fine," Stanley says, as he passes us on his way to the kitchen, with a tub of dirty dishes. "I'll keep an eye on her, Lou."

"At least let me try, Mr. Santoro? Grams thinks it will be good for me..."

Truth is, Grams is right. I need to get out into the world. I'm sixteen, and with the exception of school and home, I don't know much about anything. I'm afraid that if I don't do something with myself soon, I'm going to end up being the 'old maid' you read about, with nothing but a bunch of cats to show for my life.

So, Lou ends up giving me a chance. I start out working the register, and eventually, get to wait tables too. And, I quickly discover that Lou is right – some of the customers are... well...

Papa Roni's is stuck back in the corner of a small strip mall, near the intersection of S. College and W. Drake Roads, about a half mile from Colorado State University. While there are some college kids who come in, the place is more of a high school hang out. Rocky Mountain High is less than a mile from us. About two miles further east is FCHS. For years, each school has tried to lay claim to the restaurant as 'their place'.

Lou is all for it – as long as they are buying pizza...

Once I started working at the restaurant, Stanley and I became pretty good friends, and eventually, I discovered he's a musician. He's a keyboard player – a really good one actually. It didn't take long for me to meet Willie – he's Stanley's drummer – and by default, is my friend too.

Willie, however, is even more withdrawn than I am – if that's even possible – and so far, I haven't been able to figure out why. Sometimes, he just turns up at the restaurant and sits in a corner – alone. I usually give him a soda, and pay for it out of my tips. It seems all he does is watch people.

On the nights he shows up, he and Stanley will sit on the small stage and write songs. I usually tend to closing things up while they are playing. Sometimes, they play over songs from the jukebox, and I'm amazed at how precise they are.

You are going to hear me talk about fate and destiny a lot – as I am convinced they are in total control of our lives. Too many weird things have happened to me in my short life, for there to be any other realistic explanation.

Anyhow, on a Friday night, right after we close, one of those weird things happens. Stan and Willie are jamming away, and I'm counting money and putting it into the safe. When I stand up, I see a girl standing at the door, looking in. She has pigtails, some really interesting glasses, and appears to be trying to see where the music is coming from. I stop what I'm doing, walk over and open the door...

"We're closed... sorry."

"Oh... I didn't want anything to eat," she replies, with the most insanely hard to understand accent, I have ever heard. "I was just listening to them..." she points at Stan and Willie.

I look around and not seeing anyone other than her, I shrug and pull the door open.

"Well... come in and listen then..."

"Seriously?" she blurts out.

I laugh, and she instantly blushes.

"I'm sorry... you just sound so totally cool! And yeah, I don't see why you can't come in and listen for a while."

She grabs a backpack at her feet, comes in, and takes a seat at the first table she sees. I go back and finish what I was doing. An hour later, we all leave together, and Stanley locks the door behind us. Catrin (which I discover is the Welsh version of Catherine – and explains the accent) gets on a bike and rides off in the direction of the university. Stan and Willie get into Stan's truck and head east. I too, get on a bike, and start the two mile ride to my grandmother's.

Two weeks later, Catrin again turns up at Papa Roni's – this time about an hour before we close. It's Saturday – which means open mic night. Anyone who wants to, can get on stage and sing or play. This time, however, Matt Duncan and his cronies are pretty much controlling things. Lou told us that if he gets out of hand, to just call the cops, but Stan can usually handle him.

Matt's band – if you can call them that – isn't all that bad, really. But to look at them, you'd never know it. They're 'headbangers' – that loud, obnoxious music that some people like, but that I doubt will ever really be main stream. The thing that fascinates me is, Matt can actually sing... when he wants to. Their lead guitarist – Nick Sharpe – is the only one of the bunch that looks even close to normal. I've often wondered how he even got hooked up with Matt...

Tonight, the moment Catrin walks in, her eyes go right to Nick, and it's obvious what the girl is thinking...

In addition to discovering Cadi's crush on Nick, tonight I also discover that Matt has a weak spot... *competition*. Tonight this competition is taking the form of one really short, oriental girl, whose hair is at least five different colors. The very second she walks in, Matt gets all kinds weird.

"Hey!" he yells, right in the middle a song, "Who the hell invited you?" He's pointing at her, the entire time.

She just shakes her head, and walks over to me.

"I need to get a large supreme to go, if I could please."

I'm not even sure why, but I was expecting her to have an accent – and when she doesn't, I think my face may have given me away, because she lets out a muffled laugh.

"Yes ma'am" I reply, no doubt blushing, as I write it down and slide the slip into the kitchen. "Be about fifteen minutes."

"Hey, Emily!" I hear from behind me.

I turn and find Stanley picking up the order, and nodding at the girl.

"Hey Stan," she replies. "If it's cool with you," she says, looking first at me, then turning and glancing at the stage, "I'm gonna go sit on the curb out front. Will you holler at me when it's done?"

"Why? Because of Matt?" I ask.

She just looks at me.

"No," I say, as I ring up her order. "You sit down right there, and if that jerk says a word to you, I will take care of it. $12.75, please."

She laughs, gives me $15.00 and says, "Put the rest in the tip jar." Then she turns and does exactly what I told her to.

Even as she sits down, Matt is headed toward her. I'm watching as he stops in front of her, and puts his hands on his hips.

"*Do not* say a word, Matthew Duncan."

He hesitates, turns and glances at me, and I glare at him.

"You know good and well what Lou told me to do if you cause problems. You're a customer, she's a customer. If you guys are done playing, just say 'good night' and there's the door..." I point at it while still staring at him.

Then, out of nowhere, something strange happens.

"Good night, Emma... good night, Emily..." Nick says, then grabs Matt's arm, and pushes him toward the door. Matt goes out first, Raul and Ricky follow him, but Nick pauses. He turns and glances right at Catrin, who is sitting alone, at the table nearest the door, and for the first time I can remember, the guy actually *smiles!* And of course, she smiles back.

'Interesting...' I think to myself, and smile as well.

Believe it or not, this is the first time all five members of our band are together.

Yep... that's right. Although we don't know it yet, the five of us are going to become a band...

Remember what I said about fate and destiny?

three

the interview

"So, Emily, where should we begin? How about with Cadi? It was her illness in Germany that started the sequence of events that would eventually bring the tour to a halt, right?"

"Yes, it was. She's given me permission to share the nature of her medical condition. She suffers from severe bronchial asthma, which apparently didn't really become a problem for her until she came to the States. Most of our early fans will remember that she was quite sick and coughing when we had our 'epic fail' during the Battle Of The Bands, at CSU – what seems like forever ago. She had ongoing problems with it during our first few shows – Good Morning America and at the VMA's – but being the dedicated musician she is, she refused to give into it, or tell us what was going on."

"Yes, there have been many commentaries and a lot of speculation as to what happened that night..."

The camera widens its angle to show a video of *Audio Distortion* in concert on the large monitor and the image freezes when Cadi collapses, her bass guitar still around her shoulders.

"Unfortunately," Emily continues, "the world got to watch her endure a 'spontaneous pneumothorax' – according to the doctors. Because she kept going, instead of telling us there was a problem, it caused her lung to partially collapse."

The image on the monitor changes to Cadi on a stretcher, her cheeks cover with tears and her face contorted in pain, being put into an ambulance.

"Fortunately, her parents knew she had medical issues, and just how hard-headed the girl is, so they had a specialist standing by. Because she was still a 'minor', the hospital was forced to guard her secret as well. She was hospitalized for a week, and then came back to the States with her parents, to recover. It was the last time she was onstage with *Audio Distortion*."

"And, as the world saw…"

The monitor comes back to life, displaying a different image of *Audio Distortion* in concert – with Cadi obviously absent.

"…*Audio Distortion* went on without her."

"Yes, for a while we did. We had to – due to contract issues. Besides, Cadi insisted. We got Nick to take over Cadi's bass duties. It was a struggle for all of us, mostly because without Cadi, it just didn't seem right – it didn't seem like *Audio Distortion*. But we kept going. Once we explained what happened, most fans seemed to understand. Our fans are the best…"

"Okay, so…"

A map of Europe appears on the monitor, and lines appear between cities, as they mention them.

"…you went from Berlin to Amsterdam…"

"That was the last image you showed us. The first show without Cadi, and the most difficult."

"Then, on to Zurich – and I should mention it was one of the cities where you guys were so popular, two shows were needed."

Emily smiles.

"Then, to Paris. Here's where one of the infamous 'questions' comes up."

"Did Nick fly home between the Zurich and Paris shows?"

"Uh-huh."

"Yes he did. The promoter and our producer got together and chartered a jet and sent him back on the premise he'd be back in time for the Paris show. He left right after the Zurich show, flew overnight and arrived the next morning. He was there for twenty-four hours, then flew back and met us in Paris."

"So, next question..."

Emily again smiles, and then interrupts her.

"Why?"

"Uh-huh. Although we all suspected that..."

"Yes. They were involved – since shortly after they met. Because everyone – including the press – wanted to make such a big deal out of it, they tried to keep it to themselves. Well... that *and* Cadi's dad wasn't crazy about the idea. The band members all understood, and most of us did our best to cover them."

"Well, Emily, the world knows the two of them are no longer a 'couple'. Is this something you are willing to discuss?"

"They told me I could share whatever I want – give up all our secrets so to speak. Because the decision has been left to me, I've chosen to leave certain things in our private lives – private. There is some stuff the public simply doesn't need to know about."

"Fair enough. Let's move on. Tell us about the first concert in London and what happened with Willie."

"He melted down. Simple as that. Although they really are friends, he and Nick had this small wedge between them..."

"...named Cadi?"

Emily laughs.

"Yeah, named Cadi. Willie is the kind of guy who has a terrible time with change, and letting go of things. From the day we started the band, Cadi always made it clear, we are – and would always be – *friends*. Poor Willie felt otherwise, and it was hard for him once Nick and Cadi became a couple. He knew why Nick flew home, and it kept eating at him. When the reporter at the interview asked his question, it all caught up with Willie, and he vented. We've all done it at one point or another in our lives – Willie's meltdown just happened to be public. Hazards of being 'famous' I suppose..."

Donna shuffles some papers and continues.

"According to records, Willie publicly apologized to the reporter, as well as to all your fans. Yet despite all the publicity, the following night, you guys managed to give yet another monster performance."

"Yep. Unbeknownst to the world, just before the second London show, Willie and Nick made peace with each other. To this day, no one knows what was said between them – in fact, when we found out they were in the same dressing room together, thirty minutes before the show, we almost panicked. Emma actually started to cry. Fifteen minutes before show time, they came out, hugged each other, looked at Stan, Emma, me, and our road producer, and said 'Let's go out there and kick their as...' ...oops, I mean butts. Sorry."

Donna laughs, and pulls a sheet of paper out of the stack on her lap.

"Rolling Stone said – and this is a quote – '*...easily the most powerful show to date, for the phenomenon the world is calling Audio Distortion'.*"

"I agree. And in truth, the only way we could ever top that show, would be with Cadi."

Donna turns to face the nearest camera.

"We have to take a break, but stick with us as we continue to explore 'the phenomenon the world *called Audio Distortion*'."

The director yells "We are out! Thirty seconds!"

Donna turns to face Emily.

"We – but me most of all – were all utterly shocked when you called, Emily. Under the circumstances, I think it's one of the boldest things I've ever seen a group of young performers do – willingly sharing the secrets of their lives like this."

"So many people supported us while we were 'riding the wave', so we decided – as a band – that it was only fair we come clean with them. All of them. Even though we don't think our lives are all that important, apparently there are some fans out there that do."

"The rest of this," Donna says, holding up the pages that are in her lap, "is going to be... well..."

"Yeah, I know. And it's cool... honest. You ask, I'll answer as best I can."

"THIRTY SECONDS!" is heard through the studio speakers and once again the entire set goes quiet.

Donna stands up, steps over to Emily, leans over and gives her a hug.

"You are, in your own way, a very amazing young woman, Emily Táo."

"I'll second that," the nearest camera man offers, smiling and winking.

"FIVE... FOUR... THREE... TWO..."

four

the beginning

Emma Greene

Sitting on a stool at my kitchen counter, I'm gently scratching Jasper – she's the cat Stan gave me, to keep me company – behind the ears, while Emily's interview, is in a commercial.

So, while they are selling cars, and health club memberships, how about if we get back to *Audio Distortion's* beginnings…

*****

Over the course of a month, we learned a good bit about each other.

Emily Táo is of Chinese decent. Her family's roots – and her grandparents – are in China. Her biological mother died from complications of giving birth to her, and when she was four, the woman she has always known as Mom married her dad. She has twin siblings – a boy and girl. They are actually one of the closest families I have ever met. The interesting thing about Emily – and totally explains Matt's problem with her – is that she's a guitarist. A *really good one*, actually. There are already three decent bands at RMHS, and the last thing Matt needs, is her joining one of them. Or worse, starting a new one. Emily found it amazing that my 'cute, prim and proper' self actually stood up to Matt that night in the restaurant. A friendship that will last years, started that night.

Catrin Meredith – who told us we had to call her Cadi – also joined our band of misfits. She is indeed from Wales, and her father teaches European Culture at Colorado State. She's studying classical music there as well. She plays a number of string instruments, but the cello is her passion. The first time I watched her pick up and play a guitar, my stunned expression made *everyone* crack up. And, as it turns out, she's the oldest of us, and has already finished the British version of high school. We all find it more than amusing that Emily always seemed to be telling her to 'talk slowly'.

Willie Morgan is part Native American, and part Irish. His father was pure blood Ute and his mother was born in Ireland. Because his parents were never legally married, Willie has always carried his mom's surname – which is weird to most, because you can tell with just one look, he's Native American. Willie's shy, withdrawn thing started when his father was killed in an accident on the Reservation. While the tribal members did everything they could to help him and his mom, she eventually went back to her family. Since then, poor Willie seems caught between two cultures, not at all sure where he fits. He finally confessed that the reason he started hanging out at Papa Roni's was because he could sit in a corner and the world left him alone. Well... except for me...

Once the five of us became friends, we made a standing date, to meet every Saturday night at Papa Roni's. Once we closed, Stanley and the others would jam together, while I tended to closing things up. Lou, of course, trusted us, and never said anything about it.

However, on the night our crazy journey actually started, fate and destiny were working on a Friday...

"How long are you guys gonna be?" I ask, clearing some dishes from one of the tables.

"You don't close for another hour..." Cadi says, in her totally undecipherable accent, books spread out all over the table she is at.

Stanley shakes his head and says, "Yeah... but we'd still like to clean up and get out as early as we can."

"Well..." comes from the only other occupied table, "... if we aren't going to play tonight, I'll cut out now."

We turn to find Willie standing up, putting his backpack over his shoulder, and heading for the door. Halfway there, we hear the door chime, and when we look, find Emily coming in.

"Hey! Sorry for last minute-ing you, but my mom wants to know if you by chance have a pizza we can get to go?"

"Nope. Sorry..." Stanley blurts out.

I shake my head, give Stanley a dirty look, and as she turns to leave, say, "Hey! Hang on."

About this time, Crazy Willie (that's what a lot of people call him, because he never says much, and he's always pounding on things with his drumsticks) starts playing on the table tops, mostly because he knows it drives me nuts. Emily turns to look back at me, and then looks at Willie.

"The buffet," I turn and point at it, "still has six or seven slices on it. You want them?"

Emily turns and looks at me again.

"Seriously?"

"Yeah. We'll just toss them when we close."

"I'll pay you for them," she says, sticking her hand into the pocket of her jeans.

"It's okay – don't sweat it," I reply, grabbing a box, and putting the slices in it. "And will you *please* knock that off, Willie!"

"Well then, I'm going to play the real ones..." he says, turning and heading for the small stage at the front of the restaurant.

In seconds, Stanley stops working, and I hear keyboards just that fast. I shake my head and laugh, knowing exactly what the two of them are going to do – what they always do when the place is empty. You see, they truly love music, but because we tend to move outside the lines of normal teenagers, they've never really been able to get a band together – but then, they never really put much effort into it either.

They've been content to let music be a hobby.

But, in a matter of seconds, that's going to change.

And... it's going to be an effortless transition.

The four of them have been playing together on and off for over a month, but it's always been more about messing around, and covering songs – mostly from the jukebox – than it was about *creating*.

For the second time, fate and destiny are about to rearrange our lives. *All five of them...*

I'm closing up the box of slices, when I hear, what at the moment, seems weird. A guitar has joined Stan and Willie. When I turn to hand Emily the box of pizza, she isn't there. I turn a little further, and find her *on the stage,* and realize that she's ad-libbing right along with Stan and Willie.

Ad-libbing is the key word in that last sentence. For the first time they aren't 'covering' anything, but are instead, making it up on the fly, and it sounds *amazing!* Then, to increase the amusement and insanity of the moment, I watch our favorite college student stand up, join the others on the stage, pick up the bass guitar, and add a rhythm that almost seems to have been written for what the others are making up!

I laugh, shake my head, put the pizza box on the counter, pick up the tub of dirty dishes Stanley left, and head for the kitchen.

Thirty seconds later, fate and destiny reach out and pull *me* into the craziness. As I am putting dishes into the huge dishwasher, I realize that what they're playing actually sounds like a real song, and within seconds, my mind is putting lyrics to it. It's something I wrote a couple weeks earlier, while Stan and Willie were playing alone. The bizarre thing is, their tempo seems to *perfectly* match the words in my head, and before I realize it, I'm singing...

On a quiet night
I was cleaning tables
Watching the band
Knowing they're able

I close the dishwasher, set it to run, and just keep singing...

Wondering when
Their time will come
Wondering when
The world will notice

I turn, push the swinging door to go out into the restaurant, and find about fifteen people – *including Emily's mom*, who was waiting for her in the car – filling the place! They're clapping, tapping their feet, and listening, as Stan, Cadi, Willie and Emily, keep ad-libbing. *Everyone* turns to look at me, and I suddenly realize that *I'm still singing...*

We're here!
Night after night
We're here!
Under the lights
Hoping we'll get noticed...

And in this instant, *Audio Distortion* is born...

five

acceptance

Emma Greene

It probably wasn't fair to ignore Emily when she tried to talk to me about doing the interview, but she and I got pretty close after we lost Cadi on tour, and I somehow knew that she'd interpret my silence as 'permission' – not that she technically needs it.

Anyhow, the music world pretty much put *Audio Distortion* on the back burner when I 'slipped into oblivion' well over a year ago. For months after I disappeared from the tour, the press spent a lot of time discussing my various 'mental states'.

You see, right in the middle of our tour, God took my grandmother. At the time, the general consensus within the press seemed to be, the loss of Grams somehow made me 'crazy'.

Yeah... okay. Gotta love tabloids.

Fortunately for me, Mr. Campbell and Logan – Stan's stepmom – stepped up. Fact is, at the time, I was still a minor, and the courts become involved.

You see, *Grams* was my legal guardian, and since I was five, has raised me.

When I finally appeared in court, Stanley's dad and Logan told the judge that not only was I quite sane, but that I was also completely capable of taking care of myself. Being seventeen, I could have been emancipated by the court, but to make things easier, Logan agreed to be my legal guardian.

Because everyone at school knew what happened on tour, I chose not to go back for my senior year. With Logan's help, I got a tutor and finished at home, eventually getting my diploma.

So, my 'withdrawal'...

In reality, I wasn't as depressed, as I was *angry*. I felt – for quite a while – that God had cheated me. I let go of music completely. Truth is, I didn't *want* to sing. The night I lost Grams, I also lost the desire to share my voice. I felt that the trade-off of having the gift of a voice wasn't equal to the price required – giving up my family. And... if I couldn't have my family, I simply wasn't going to share my gift anymore.

Now that the dust has settled, my friends have taken the position that I'm probably *afraid* to sing again, because I haven't in so long. During our few, brief, conversations, Stanley *always* asks the same question – *'have you exercised those vocal chords lately?'* – and each time, the only response I give him, is a strange look.

But over time, something inside me (I like to call it 'destiny') kept pushing, and pushing, and after six months, I realized the anger was gone , and had been replaced by uncertainty, and the knowledge that my 'gift' was all I had left.

So, I started singing again – to Jasper. She's my 'audience of one'.

Now, as I sit listening to Donna Dollar welcome her viewers back, I know deep down, that fate and destiny are once again about to stick their big noses back into my life – *into all our lives* – just like they did years ago, in a laid-back pizza parlor, in Fort Collins, Colorado.

six

the interview

"Welcome back," Donna says, taking her seat and again facing Emily. "For those of you just joining us, Emily Táo, original lead guitarist for *Audio Distortion*, is here today talking with me about the band's rise and fall. So Emily, having lived it yourself, I don't need to tell you that the next part of this outline, truly astounded me. Ready to discuss what was described by most news agencies at the time, as *'the total collapse of the year's best new band'*?"

"Sure. Most of the world is aware that Emma has sort of become a recluse. When I said earlier that I'd spoken to 'almost everyone' it was a reference to not having talked to Emma."

"I think the biggest question about Emma is – was her withdrawal due to the loss of her grandmother, or her breakup with Stan?"

"Actually, neither of those is a fair explanation of what happened to Emma Greene. If any member of the band had a legitimate reason to bail, it was Emma – and none of us would have blamed her. But disbanding wasn't her idea. Emma's story – as best I know it – is actually a very sad one."

Emily pauses, picks up a bottle of water from a table next to her, uncaps it, and takes a long, slow drink. After a few seconds of contemplation, she sets the bottle and cap back on the table, and faces Donna.

"Yes, she and Stanley were a couple, and I believe it was good for both of them. She gave Stan purpose, and he gave her direction. Together they're an unstoppable writing team, and were the core of *Audio Distortion*'s music. Anyhow, when Emma's grandmother passed, it went public – and yes, Emma went completely to pieces emotionally. Thing is, no one knew the real reason."

"So there were mitigating circumstances?"

"Yeah. A really big one actually. One that she had to make herself share with us – meaning the members of the band."

"You've mentioned twice now, that you haven't been in contact with Emma recently…"

"In close to a year actually. Stan is the only one she talks to even semi-regularly."

"Are you certain that what you are about to tell us, is something she wants out there? The last thing I want to do on this show, is to cause her undue stress, by invading her privacy. That's not what I'm about."

"No one in the band can answer that question – except Emma. Stan told her what I planned to do, but she gave him no response. While she didn't give me permission to discuss this, she didn't say I couldn't either. I guess it comes down to how I choose to interpret her silence. But the band members feel we need to set the record straight and make sure the world knows there are real and very sincere reasons for her behavior. She isn't crazy – which is what some of the tabloids want everyone to believe."

"Well, go ahead then, Emily. Tell us."

"We were nearing the end of the tour – only eight shows left. We managed to trudge through without Cadi, and our fans responded so positively that we couldn't have stopped. That's when Emma finally got us together – me, Stan, Willie, and Nick – and told us what had happened. You see, Donna, only a month before Grams died, so did her father."

The entire set becomes eerily quiet, and Donna turns an interesting shade of pale.

"Her... *father*?" Donna almost forces out.

"Yes. That's what the world never knew. When all of you – meaning reporters and tabloid hounds – assumed that her grandmother raised her because *both* of her parents were killed in an accident, she found it easier not to correct you. Only her mother died when she was young."

"But... she lived with... where was..." Donna mumbles, visibly confused.

"Yes, she lived with her grandmother – since she was five. Would you like to know why?"

"This is going beyond what the producers prepared me for, Emily. Before you go any further, there is something I personally need to do."

"Sure."

Donna turns and looks directly at the camera nearest her, takes a deep breath, and says, "Emma, if you are out there, and are by chance watching this, please... please, call the studio and tell us if you want this out there. I don't know what it may be..."

In the middle of her speech, the terse silence of the studio is suddenly pierced by a strange ringtone, and everyone starts checking their cell phones – assuming they'd forgotten to silence theirs. Emily, immediately recognizing the ring, knows it is hers.

"It's mine, everyone," Emily says. "I'm sorry – I forgot to turn it off." She stands and looks at one of the stage hands, and asks, "Do you know what they did with my backpack? I laid it over there."

A young girl comes across the room, the ringing backpack in her hands. Everyone is so caught up in the moment, that no one thinks to go to break, and the cameras keep rolling – *live*. Emily digs out her phone and after glancing at the caller ID, shrugs and flips it open.

Destiny and fate – the two things that brought them all together the first time, years ago, is again about to step in.

"This is Emily…"

seven

conceding

Emma Greene

The moment Emily tells them about my dad, I know what needs to be done. I owe her at least that much. I can't even imagine how much stress she's under at this exact moment – knowing she agreed to tell the entire truth, about all of us.

I grab my phone, and autodial Emily, as I walk into the living room and plop down on the couch. I actually laugh as I watch the confusion my call creates on the set. 'Strange' I think to myself, just as Emily answers, 'no one thought to go to commercial?'

"This is Emily."

"It's me, Em…"

"Wow… you *are* watching. How freakin' weird is that?"

"Not very, if you think about it. You're about to give away all of our secrets – no way would I miss that," I quickly reply. "And, for the record, you can tell them whatever you want."

"Are you sure, Emma?"

"Yeah, Emily… I am. It's probably time."

"Okay… if you're sure."

"I am. And I'm watching too – so keep that in mind."

"Will you call me back later this evening?"

"We'll see... one step at a time."

"Okay. Talk to you later... I hope. Bye."

"Bye."

In this single moment, I feel some kind of strange release – as if everything that's been complicating my existence for the last two years suddenly evaporates. I lay the phone on the table, let Jasper jump into my lap, and turn my attention to the TV...

eight

the interview

As Emily closes her phone and turns around, it dawns on her that she is now the center of attention in the studio. She smiles, shakes her head, walks back over to the set and takes her seat.

"Let me guess…" Emily says, nodding at the camera nearest them, "live means *live*?"

"Uhh…"

"Doesn't matter. This whole thing was about the truth anyhow, right?"

Donna nods her agreement.

"Well, as you all just heard, I got permission from the last remaining member of *Audio Distortion*, to finish this story. You ready?"

Silence. It's as if none of them – least of all Donna Dollar – can believe what's happening, let alone that it's happening live in front of them.

"Emma's dad was institutionalized. She told us about it, one night at the pizzeria, a month after we met. As she put it to us that day, *'…he felt responsible for her mother's death, and it was more than he could take'.* He apparently slipped into his own world, and when he tried to take his own life, the doctors felt it best to commit him."

Emily reaches to her side, picks up her bottle of water and again takes a sip from it. Then, with a big grin, she points at a guy who is frantically waving his arms and looks like he might faint any moment.

"Donna, I think your producer is trying to get your attention."

Donna turns and after a quick glance at the arm-waving guy, realizes what is going on, and turns back to the camera.

"Well... Emily is right. We need to take a break – and after that last revelation, I know I can use one. Stick with us, we'll be right back."

"We are out – *finally*! Thirty seconds people."

"Was that really Emma? The call I mean..."

"Yeah, it was. Fate, destiny, karma. Maybe all of them combined. Years ago, Mrs. Dreesen said it was destiny that brought us together that night at Papa Roni's. And if you think about it, how else can you explain five totally different, musically inclined kids, who really didn't know each other, ending up alone in a pizza parlor? What if my mom, hadn't wanted a pizza that night..."

Emily lifts the bottle and takes another sip.

"And... how do we explain *this?* Not a peep out of her for close to a year, yet she *is* watching this, and realizing what I am about to do, calls me. I mean, whose idea was it to do this live – instead of taping it?"

"TEN SECONDS!" rings out across the studio.

After a third sip from the bottle, Emily caps it and sets it back down on the table.

"This all means something, Donna, I'm just not sure what yet. You ready to finish this?"

"Uh... yeah... I suppose. I'm so overwhelmed at the moment, Emily, that it may as well be your show at this point."

Emily laughs as the stage manager starts counting.

"FIVE... FOUR... THREE... TWO..."

"Welcome back to the strangest show I have so far hosted. I'm not sure about the rest of you, but in the last thirty minutes, my entire concept and image of *Audio Distortion* has been changed. So many revelations... so quickly."

"So," Emily says, pulling her feet up under her in the chair, her attitude and demeanor seeming to change, "call it quits, or finish the story?"

"The floor is yours, young lady."

"I'll finish with Emma's story, and then tell you what we have each been doing since we let *Audio Distortion* go, a year ago. Fair?"

"Perfect!" Donna replies.

"Well, as I was saying, Emma's dad was killed – it happened in the institution. It was a fluke accident – a once in a million years kinda thing. It happened the day we played our last US concert in Seattle, although none of us knew it. Richard – our producer – snuck up to Emma's room after the show, and privately gave her a sealed letter than had been over-nighted to her by Grams. Not even he knew what was in it, but he had to assume it was bad news of some kind. She waited until he was gone before reading it, and for whatever reason, decided to keep her dad's death to herself. The next day, we flew to Rome and started the European leg of our tour, and seeing Emma, you wouldn't have known anything was wrong. She was the gung-ho, hell-bent, frontman for *Audio Distortion*, and nothing was going to change that. For the next thirty-one days, she kept the tour rolling, night after night, show after show."

Emily again stops talking, and sits quietly staring off into the darkness of the studio. It's apparent she is remembering... Fifteen seconds elapses before, with her gaze still locked on the darkness, she continues.

"We were backstage in Madrid when the news about Grams reached us. Why Richard didn't wait until after the show to give Emma the message, will always be a mystery. Anyhow, we all stood and watched Emma read the message from my mom, waiting for her to faint, or cry… or anything. Instead, the girl forced a smile, looked right at us and said, 'Let's go guys – they've made enough noise that we owe them an encore, right?' Believe it or not, Emma sang *A Hard Road* with more passion that night, than she ever had. It was amazing…"

As Emily again reaches for her water, Donna shuffles through her stack of pages, and pulls out another single page.

"I'm going to read the statement issued by Rolling Stone concert reporter Randy Rogers the night you guys did that show…

> *'…and tonight I saw what I believe was the best encore in the history of pop music encores. Having lost their bass player, vocalist, and good friend, Cadi, five weeks ago in Berlin, Emily and Emma have since then, been covering all her vocals – and according to fans I've spoken to, are doing a beautiful job of it.*
>
> *Tonight in Madrid, however, the band's frontman took over. As Stan Campbell played the intro to A Hard Road, Emma Greene managed to quiet an arena full of screaming kids, long enough to tell them that her grandmother had passed away, and that their encore tonight was dedicated to her. Then, as the other members of Audio Distortion took turns hugging her, mic still in hand, Emma added this – 'you all know the words to this song, so in memory of Grams, I hope all of you will sing with me…'*

That, readers, was all it took to create the greatest live performance of A Hard Road...'"

Once Donna finishes reading, she sits staring at the page in her hand, as if unsure what to say or do next. The eerie silence is eventually broken when Emily, whose face is still covered by a look of deep contemplation, takes a huge breath, turns and looks directly at the camera.

"Right here, on me, please. I need to be sure Emma hears and understands what I am about to say."

The guy on the camera immediately complies with Emily's request – as if she is the director. The camera pans slightly, centers on her and then zooms to fill the screen with her face. The continuing silence is so acute, that the only sound heard is the hum of all the electronic equipment.

"Two years ago, Cadi and I wrote a song, just to see if we could do it. It's a song that *Audio Distortion* never played live, and that was recorded only once, as an added track for the CD. It's our song – *the band's*. You know exactly what I'm talking about, Emma. We've played it as a band only twice – the first time, under that tree in your backyard, and the second was in the studio the day we recorded it. The four of us – Cadi included – want you to know that we are ready to meet you in Gram's backyard, under that same tree, and sing it again. We're just waiting for you to tell us you are ready."

When she finally stops talking, the tears on her cheeks are blatantly visible. She reaches for the water, uncaps it, and finishes what's in the bottle. With one hand she wipes the tears off her face and with the other, flings the empty bottle across the set, and laughs.

"Now, would you like to know about the rest of *Audio Distortion?*"

Donna nods her agreement, without speaking.

"Stan is back in school, at CSU. He plans to major in music, but will also get his teaching degree. He's been helping his old music teacher, Mrs. Dreesen – the woman who sorta pushed us into all this – on a regular basis, when his class schedule permits. He's also been writing music for other artists, and even for movies. Every so often our paths cross – usually when I need his help. I believe that in his heart, he hopes to one day recapture the magic he and Emma shared – both musically, and emotionally."

She hesitates for a second, then again turns to face the nearest camera.

"Yeah, Stanley, that's right... I said it. Sue me."

She stands up, and with a laugh asks, "Is there another bottle of water I can have?"

Within seconds a number of full, cold, bottles of water sail onto the set from different directions, forcing Emily to dodge them. She breaks up in laughter as she picks them up, knowing the crew did it in an attempt to relax things. Once she has them all, she sets them on the table, and then takes her seat.

"As the world knows, Cadi moved back to England. Even before the tour crashed, her parents found a specialist there who agreed to work with her," she continues, opening one of the bottles, and taking a huge drink. "Shortly after we all got back here, Cadi's father was offered a teaching position over there, and went to join his family. The doctors say that living in the country, on an island, is the best thing for Cadi's medical issues for now. She still loves music, and she plays regularly with a small orchestra – the classical music she was studying when Stan and I originally hijacked her into *Audio Distortion*. She's also tried her hand at acting, as most Brits will know, turning up in a few episodes of their most popular daytime drama. And, she isn't half bad, if I do say so.

"Nick. Well... he couldn't live without rocking out. It's just in the guy's blood. When we finally threw in the towel, he went in search of a new band. It wasn't at all personal – the guy just *needed* to make music. After months of drifting around LA, being unable to find anywhere he fit, he too, ended up back in Fort Collins. And, as a lot of people know, within weeks of getting home, he managed to reform our old nemesis, *Always Louder*. Matt and Raul were going to CSU, and Nick has enrolled as well. They found a new drummer, and a management company, and have started playing gigs at smaller, more personal venues, when their school schedules permit. Time changes everything, and in some instances, can even heal old wounds. He and Matt are both different people now – better people. And, as hard as it is for me to admit, *Always Louder* has even used my facility – Discovery Studios – a couple of times.

"Willie Morgan – the mad percussionist. He and I work together almost every day. And before you tabloid freaks get started, we are, and will always be, just really good friends. For lack of anything better to do at the time, and with Mr. Campbell's help, we invested most of our 'amassed fortune' and started Discovery Studios – a small set-up designed to help out kids like we once were. Curious and interested, but struggling, with no direction. To support what we do with the kids, we do a lot of session work, playing back up for some known, and some yet undiscovered artists, when they need us. We both still love to play, and even though a studio isn't a stage, it works for us. I should point out that, although Nick and company used the studio, I drew the line at playing back-up for them, on principle."

Her comment causes an eruption of laughter.

"Music fans, the laughter you just heard *is not* an audience, as today this is a closed set. *That*..." Donna says, fighting off a laugh, and shaking her head, "was the show's crew and support team."

"For the most part, Donna," Emily continues, "the last year of our lives has been spent visiting high schools all over the country, talking to music teachers and students, and searching for the next *Audio Distortion*. We haven't found them yet, but Willie and I believe they're out there, somewhere, waiting for that one push. The same push Mrs. Maxwell gave the five of us, one fateful Sunday afternoon, in a pizza parlor."

Emily falls silent, appearing to be lost in thought. She reaches for one of the water bottles, and then changes her mind, setting it back down, and again looking at Donna.

"So there you have it – what really happened to *Audio Distortion*, and where we are now. Not all that exciting, but at least it's all true."

"Amazing. Totally amazing. I feel honored that you chose my show to set the record straight, Emily. We need to take one last break, then, with your permission, the producer has agreed to let us take a few calls, to see what your fans have to say about all this. Music fans... please come back – you don't want to miss the end of this show."

"We're out! We over-shot, so this is a short one, people. Twenty seconds."

"Are you up to taking the calls, Emily? If you aren't we can always claim technical difficulties you know. I just wanted to get it out before the break so that if anyone did want to call, they would."

Emily is about to answer when a booming voice fills the entire studio.

"Jeezzz! They've buried the freaking switchboard, Donna!"

That is quickly followed by, "TEN SECONDS!"

Emily laughs, and with a smile says, "I guess the fans are deciding for me, Donna. Let's do this!"

As the seconds tick down, a girl with a clipboard comes running across the studio, slides to a stop next to Donna and, almost out of breath, hands her the pages on the clipboard. Donna scans them, laughs, and hands the pages back.

"Care to guess what the BIG question is, Emily? What every person who has called so far has asked?"

"FIVE... FOUR... THREE... TWO..."

nine

acceptance

Emma Greene

The moment Emily mentions *We Are*, I almost burst into tears. She's sending me a message – one that I need to pay attention to, and I know it.

Then, when Donna mentions taking calls, I have the most insane idea, and know that if I can make myself do it, it will help Emily out, tremendously.

Even as the butterflies in my stomach take flight, I pick up my phone and dial the studio number, which has been scrolling across the bottom of the screen since they went to commercial.

Busy signal.

I sit staring blankly a car commercial, and after about ten seconds, try again.

Same result – busy signal. Apparently, a lot of fans have a lot to say.

I watch as the show returns from commercial, yet nothing happens. The camera is in a wide shot of Donna and Emily doing nothing except staring at each other – silently.

"Well, Jasper, there's always more than one way to accomplish most tasks, and these two look like they need something to talk about..."

My heart now racing, I again, autodial Emily's number. It only takes her two rings.

"Yeah?"

"If you want some help, no questions asked, hand the phone to Donna."

I hear her laugh, there's a brief silence, and then I hear Donna.

"Hello?"

"Hey, Donna... Guess who?"

"NO WAY!"

I laugh.

"I assure you it's me, and because *everyone* knows you like to 'color outside the lines' so to speak, I have a little proposition for you. I'll give you an honest answer to one question *on air*, if you'll let me say something I think needs to be said. If you are up for it, hand the phone back to Emily and I will tell her what needs to be done. If not, then just hang up, and I'll understand. Either way, thanks for letting Emily share our story with the world."

The woman is so quiet, I find myself wondering if she's still breathing. The only way I can tell she's still with me, is because I'm watching her head going up and down, in a comical way, on TV. Then, without a word, I watch her hand the phone to Emily.

"Yeah?" Emily says.

"Lay the phone down, and put a mic next to it. She gets to ask me one question on-air, and then I get to say something."

"You got it."

"I figured you could use some help..."

"Under the circumstances, it can't hurt. And for the record, Emma, you are – and always will be – our *only* frontman."

I watch quietly, my heart now speeding out of control, as Emily does as I request, and once they're ready, speaks to Donna.

"Okay, Donna, go ahead, ask the same question you did during the break," Emily says.

As it turns out, the question Donna asked off-air is in fact, the one thing I want to talk about...

Once again, fate and destiny are playing with us.

ten

the interview

Donna doesn't do the standard 'welcome back' intro this time. The whole interview has gone way past 'standard' at this point. Even though she knows the cameras are rolling, and it is a *live* show, she just sits grinning at Emily, as if waiting for her to answer the question she posed off camera. Everyone in the studio is holding their collective breath, and you can feel the tension, when once again, that same bizarre ringtone breaks the silence. Emily and Donna start laughing, as Emily reaches over, picks up her phone, answers it, and then promptly hands it to Donna.

"It's for you this time."

Donna reaches over, takes the phone, and with a quizzical look, places it to her ear.

"Hello? NO WAY!"

Donna is so shocked that it takes every ounce of her willpower to maintain her composure. She sits listening, her head going up and down as if in acknowledgement of what is being said, and finally, she pulls the phone from her ear and hands it back to Emily. Still smiling, Emily puts it to her ear.

"Yeah? You got it. Under the circumstances, it can't hurt. And for the record, Emma, you are – and always will be – our *only* frontman."

Emily turns, looks over at the nearest equipment person and says, "I need a mic, please?" Then she puts the phone on speaker, and lays it on the table next to her. Ten seconds later, there is a small wireless mic lying next to it.

"Okay, Donna, go ahead, ask the same question you did during the break," Emily says, a devious grin covering her face.

"Music fans, I asked Emily if she knew what BIG question is occupying the minds of *Audio Distortion*'s fans – the question that was asked by every single one of the first 100 people who called the studio line during the break."

A soft and slightly shaky voice is heard over the studio speakers, and on TVs around the world.

"They, and you too, Donna, probably want to know if the five of us will ever be on stage together again."

"Yes, Emma, that's the question. Will the *original members* of *Audio Distortion* – those five kids who took the world by storm – ever play together again?"

"Well, Donna, since this all started, I've learned a number of things that I wouldn't otherwise have. Mrs. Dreesen taught me to believe in my destiny – to accept it, and to follow it. Stan taught me to have faith in myself. Emily, in her own weird way, taught me that it was okay to let out the inner me – to simply be Emma. And Grams... she taught me that nothing is impossible. She always told me that things that might *seem* impossible, simply require more effort to accomplish. My answer to you – and to all the *Audio Distortion* fans – is this... *nothing is impossible, especially if you believe it can be done*. Donna, I know you are probably over your show's time, but well... thanks for letting me say that."

"Crap! Are you kidding me?" Donna suddenly blurts out, completely losing her composure. "Half the televisions in the country are tuned into this right now. Not even the network is foolish enough to..."

"AND WE ARE OUT! MAN... what a show!" comes blasting through the speakers, filling the studio, as the entire crew breaks into applause and cheers.

eleven

intent

Emily Tao

I'm halfway to Tahoe – where I now live – when my phone rings. A glance at the caller ID tells me who it is, and I hit the Bluetooth button on the stereo.

"Hey, Willie!"

Instead of Willie's voice, I hear Stan.

"Back when I first met you, Emily, I knew you were crazy. It just took me some time find out how crazy..."

"YOU FREAKIN' ROCK, EM!" I hear Willie add, and realize they're conferencing.

"I'm confused guys, am I in trouble or what?"

"You were perfect, Emily. None of us could have handled that better," Stan replies.

"Stan wants us to fly over and visit next week," Willie interjects.

"All these kids know about me... about us. After your little dissertation on TV, I'm hoping you guys might consider coming over – if your schedule allows – and speak at the school. You up for that?"

"I'm always up for visiting you, and Mrs. Dreesen. When do we need to be there?"

"Say, Thursday next week? If you guys get a flight into Municipal, I can pick you up, and you can crash at my house if you want. I know my dad, Logan, and Georgie would love to see you guys."

"Well... considering my sister has taken over my room at my parents' house, I might take you up on the lodging offer, but I think I'm going to make Willie drive that expensive car of his. It'll take us a couple of days, but I need some 'down time' anyhow."

"Woo Hoo! Road trip!" Willie blurts out.

"Okay then... see you guys in a week. Drive safely, Willie!"

"Stan... wait. What about..."

"I don't know Em... I don't know. She isn't answering her phone, and although I thought about going over, I've learned it's usually best to just give her some time. I couldn't believe she actually called you, to be honest. We'll talk, and maybe go knock on her door, when you guys get here, okay?"

"Fair enough. But if you hear from her, you'd better call me..."

"I will. Later guys."

I hear him hang up, and then I speak to Willie.

"I'll be back at the studio around midnight. We don't have anything going on in the morning, so do you want to go to breakfast?"

"Sure. Call me when you are ready. Drive safe, Emily. Bye."

"Bye," I reply, then reach up and push the Bluetooth button, disconnecting the phone.

I have another two hours of driving ahead of me... and lots of time to think.

twelve

panic

Emma Greene

Being in the 'limelight' – even briefly – gave me a rush I haven't had since I ran away from the tour.

It takes a full hour for my heart to slow down again, during which time I do nothing but sit on the couch, and stare blankly at the TV... thinking.

Even though Stanley called twice right after the show, I couldn't make myself answer. I know he is concerned, and worries about me, but my heart and mind just aren't ready for him yet. Instead, my brain is filled with a single thought...

What did I just start? More importantly, *why* did I start it?

Destiny?

All I know for certain is, it *needed* to be done...

Feeling the need to write, I head for the basement, with Jasper following close behind. At around 1:00 AM, as I sit staring at a jumbled mess of blurry words on a page, the phone on the wall rings, and pretty much weirds me out. You see, the important people call my cell, which leaves no explanation for why the house phone would be ringing – *especially* at 1:00 AM.

Even as an intense feeling of dread sweeps over me, a different feeling – one I can't even explain – makes me stand up, walk over, and answer it.

"Hello?"

"Oh thank goodness! Someone answered. I'm sorry to wake you, but..."

The female voice at the other end explains that Emily wrecked her Jeep, and they're trying to locate her *'next of kin'*...

Uh-huh... you guessed it.

I freak.

After close to a minute of my uncontrolled sobbing, the lady – who it turns out, is a nurse – manages to get me to listen again, and explains that Emily is fine. She apologizes for her choice of words, and then asks if I am *family*.

I think it's that single question that pulls me out of the dark hole I've been in, for over a year.

Like I keep saying... *fate and destiny*.

It seems they *never* do things the easy way.

I give the nurse the Táo's home number, and she thanks me. I hang up and quickly dial Stanley's cell phone. His groggy, still-asleep, voice answers on the second ring.

"*Emma?* Are you okay?"

"Sorta. But Emily isn't..." I reply.

It takes me ten minutes to explain it all to Stan, who then wakes up his dad and puts him on the phone. Mr. Campbell explains that he'll call Emily's parents, and will have his company jet go get her, first thing in the morning. He also subtly suggests I go too – saying that a familiar face is important in situations like this.

Mr. Campbell is awesome, and has, in many ways, been my surrogate parent since I lost Grams.

At 9:00 AM the following morning, I walk into a hospital room to find a slightly bruised, and sound asleep Emily.

thirteen

the accident

Emily Taó

"Easy, Emily... deep breath," Emma says, reaching out and taking my hand.

I force myself to relax, roll my head from side to side, taking in all my surroundings, then turn back to face Emma – as my brain tries to process the question of her 'realness'.

"Why?" I mumble, indicating my surroundings.

"Deer. You need to stop driving the mountains late at night, Emily."

"Where?"

"Where did the deer end your trip, or where are you now?" she asks, actually smiling at me, which of course makes my heart race, and the heart monitor beep faster.

"Which hospital?"

"Carson Valley. You were unconscious after the accident and this is the nearest trauma center."

"Oh god... trauma center?"

"Relax, will you? The doctor says you'll be fine. Sore for a few days, but fine. Your Jeep, however, is another story. I hope you aren't attached to it."

She smiles at me a second time, and somehow I know it's a sincere smile. Then, as my mind begins to clear, a thought occurs to me – well, a couple of them actually.

First... here she is, holding my hand, and anyone witnessing it, would never realize we haven't seen, or spoken to each other – with the exception of two phone calls – in over a year.

Second... although I know the first issue should concern me, it doesn't.

Third... even though I'm lying in a hospital bed, with no memory of how I got here, seeing Emma Greene, standing there smiling, makes everything else seem totally irrelevant.

"Okay... and why are you here?" I ask, trying to mimic her intonations – as best I remember them. It's a game we all played while on tour, and it turns out I'm best at doing 'Emma'.

"Because of that stupid little card you put in your wallet – behind your driver's license. You had the same one in your passport too, as I recall..."

She's making reference to Mr. Campbell's business card, which we all took with us when we went on tour – as a precaution. Stan's dad told us that if something completely bizarre and out of our control happened, we were to call him collect, and he'd immediately fix it. Being the cocky brat I've always been, on the back of both of my cards, I wrote 'and call Grams too!' along with her phone number.

"No one answered Mr. Campbell's business phone, so the doctor called 'Grams'."

"I guess it's a good thing I'm abnormal and obnoxious, huh?"

"Fate and destiny, Emily..."

Emma is interrupted by a doctor and a police officer as they enter the room.

"I see our 'famous' patient is awake," the guy in the white coat says, picking up my chart.

"Oh jezzz…" I mumble without thinking about it, making Emma laugh. "I haven't been 'famous' in a long time, Doc…"

"Well… with a middle school and a high school within walking distance of this facility, I'm not willing to take the chance your 'fans' have forgotten you, Miss Táo. No one except me, two nurses, and," he pauses and points at the guy in uniform, "the State Police, know you are here. The last thing we need is a bunch of crazed teenagers running around the building looking for you."

Emma, the trooper, and a nurse who came in while the doctor was talking, all break up laughing.

"Sooo…" I say, looking directly at the trooper, "Am I in trouble?"

"No ma'am – not at all. I just wanted to check on you, having been the first one on the scene. The driver of the other vehicle involved, as well as one going south, gave us a full accounting of the accident. It was just one of those things, Miss Táo – inevitable, if you will. Your Jeep – or what's left of it – is at the impound lot in Carson City. Once you feel up to it, you can go and get whatever you want out of it. We won't release it to the insurance company until you tell us to. And by the way, you should thank whoever made all the modifications to it – they are probably what let you walk away from this. If it had been a stock Jeep… well…"

"Thanks. I'll have a friend go and clean it out in the next few days."

With a smile, he turns and leaves. The doctor closes my chart, puts it back in its slot, and looks at me.

"I'm going to keep you one more day – just because. After that, you can go home as long as someone is there with you, for a few days."

"I'm taking her to my house, in Fort Collins."

"Huh?" I blurt out, turning to look at Emma.

"Fair enough, Miss Greene," the doctor replies. "I'll see you again before you leave, Miss Táo."

He turns and goes out the door.

"What do you mean, 'I'm taking her to my house'?" I ask, as she sits down on the edge of the bed.

"They called – at 1:00 AM I should point out – and I have no idea what made me pick up the phone. They told me what happened and that the number for Stan's dad – *the only number they could find* – was being answer by a machine. Having found the number on the back of the card, they tried it. They asked if I knew how to contact your *'next of kin'*. I freaked, Emily... honest to God..."

I watch her face, fully understanding what she means. The last thing Emma needs is to think someone else died...

"I called Stanley," she continues, "His dad sent me here in his business jet this morning. It's at the airport in Reno waiting for us. He also called your parents. The deal is, I bring you back with me. Willie packed some of your stuff – your guitar of course – and is already on his way there. And can you tell me why your parents' number is nowhere to be found in your wallet? I mean, really, Emily..."

When she smiles, and again squeezes my hand, I find myself praying – mentally asking God if we can have Emma back now...

The Emma we coerced into joining our band of lunatics, inside a storage room, in Papa Roni's.

The Emma, whose amazing strength held us together as a band, after we lost Cadi.

The Emma, who is – and always will be – our band's only lead singer.

"It will be now…" I reply, making myself smile.

We sit staring at each other, both fully aware that our lives are once again, about to change. Neither of us has any idea how – but we know it's coming. After a few moments of deeply intense contemplation, I break the silence.

"*Fate and destiny…* As usual, you are so right, Emma."

fourteen

the story continues

Emily

It's my turn to give you a little background.

You see, while the others pretty much let me talk them into the whole 'band' thing, I'm the pushy reason *Audio Distortion* actually came to be.

I desperately wanted to be a rock star – as absurdly childish as that may sound. The really cool thing about *AD* is how four amazing people taught me that it isn't about being a star, but instead, it's *all about the music*...

Stanley and Willie are both amazingly in love with music, but they would have been content to have played at the restaurant forever. One wanted to be a teacher, and the other a sound engineer. Neither ever gave any thought to the possibility of being pop music superstars.

Catrin Meredith... Her heart was – and in many ways, still is – in classical music. But the very second the opportunity presented itself, her response was totally automatic. The girl lives for music – regardless of the form it takes.

And Emma... well... she's the 'background' I'm about to give you.

That first night we actually played together turned comical before it was over. Poor Emma completely freaked on us. She never even considered singing before that night, and doing it in front of a crowd, was more than she could deal with. She never made it to the second verse – heck, we didn't find out for about three weeks, that there was one.

Thing is, Emma's voice is so totally amazing, it stopped *everyone* in the restaurant for just a split second, the instant we heard it. Even *my mom* – who had been in the car waiting for me, and came inside to see what was going on.

The very moment Emma stopped singing, a female voice was heard over the music the four of us were still playing...

"OMG – Wait till I tell my dad we have a freakin' house band!" Maggie – Lou's youngest daughter – yelled. She pushed her way through the small crowd, and stopped right in front of a completely freaked-out Emma, and added, "Emma, you have an *amazing* voice, and your band *so totally rocks!*"

The four of us stopped playing, the restaurant fell *completely silent*, and then Emma burst into tears, and bolted back into the kitchen.

Our guitars still over our shoulders, Cadi and I jumped off the stage and quickly followed her...

"You can't stay in there all night, Emma," Cadi said, knocking on the door to the store room.

"What's the problem, girl? You sing as well as you handle Matt, for crying out loud."

Behind us, we heard Stan first, then Willie.

"The crowd was bummed," Stanley said, winking at me. "They wanted to hear the rest of the song..."

"That was amazing," the ever quiet Willie added, as Cadi and I handed him our guitars.

Stan, a big grin covering his face, stepped between us, and gently knocked on the door.

"Look, Emma – either you come out and talk to us, or I come in. I do have the keys, remember?" Stan jingled a key ring he was holding, and then laughed.

"Just talk to us, Emma..." Cadi added.

After a few seconds, we heard the lock being turned, but the door didn't open, so I opened it. Inside was the most terrified girl I'd ever seen in my life. I swear, my heart actually hurt for her...

"How you feeling, Emma?" I asked.

"Seriously?" She lifted her head and looked at me like I was crazy, which made everyone laugh.

"That's our girl!" Cadi said, renewing the laughter.

"Jezzz, Emma, what the heck is wrong?" I asked, sitting next to her on the floor.

"people... I can't do people... too many people..." she whispered, burying her head in her hands.

"That's not true," Stanley was quick to say. "I just heard fifteen people, *including Mrs. Táo*, all say the same thing – *'Can she sing, or what?'*"

"Yeah," Willie added, "and they wanted to know what our band name is..."

"I think, that decision is going to be Emma's..." I said, very calmly.

She slowly lifted her head, and as her breathing returned to normal, with a smile and tear covered cheeks, she said, "If we're gonna be a band, you guys are going to have to figure out how to get me over the whole 'crowd' thing..."

And so it began...

*****

Catrin

My turn. I'm going to explain our band name.

Three weeks after the 'incident' (that's what we all call it, mostly because it bugs Emma) I was again trying to do some homework, when Emma sat down at the table, and handed me a sheet of paper. The moment I realized they were lyrics, my heart raced. Thing is... she hadn't even mention music since she freaked on us.

It was Saturday night, and once Emily turned up, we intended to practice for a while – we being the four of us. Emma was still avoiding the stage...

"That's what I was singing..." Emma says, smiling at me. "Maybe... if you have all the words, you guys can work on it."

"Cool," I quickly reply. "Stanley got all the music down on paper, so we'll see what we can do."

Emma instantly wrinkles her face up, telling me I'm again, talking to fast. I roll my eyes, and mumble 'sorry', which makes her laugh.

"Eventually we'll..." she starts to say, but is instantly drowned out by the most bizarre sound, coming from the speakers on stage.

When we look, we see Stanley standing next to his keyboard, with the silliest smirk on his face, while Emma and I pull our fingers out of our ears.

"Jezzz Stanley!" I blurt out.

"Sorry... I didn't check the volume."

"What was that?" I turn and glance at Emma, and although she has an odd look on her face, she doesn't say anything.

"F sharp through the synthesizer... why?"

In the blink of an eye, the smirk on Emma's face spreads into a giant grin. She reaches over, grabs a sheet of paper off the stack in front of me, and starts writing – well... drawing actually. I sit quietly and watch, definitely curious. A minute later, she slides it over in front of me, and I find...

AUDIO DISTORTION

...drawn neatly across the middle of the page. The moment I see it, I know exactly what it is. With a grin, I pick up my pink eraser, carefully remove two of the letters, then take the pencil from Emma, and as she watches, draw in two small changes – just because I can. When I'm done, she looks at it, and as we break out laughing, Emily comes in the door, stops next to us, and looks over my shoulder.

"OMG! It's perfect!" she blurts out, and then joins in our laughter.

"What the heck is going on?" Stanley asks, as he and Willie start toward us.

"We *must be* a band..." I say, holding up the sheet of paper, so they can see it, "...because Emma just came up with what has to be *the most insanely cool name...*"

AUDI◉ DIST◉RTION

*****

Stanley

As long as we're doing 'background' I figure I should get in a few words about our evolution as well. After all, I am, after a fashion, the reason Emma went along with all this to begin with.

I'll bet you're probably trying to figure out how five off-the-grid kids ended up on a world tour, right?

It started at the Battle of the Bands. And although you may think it was Emily's doing, it wasn't.

It was a music teacher.

Her name is Mrs. Dressen.

She knew someone...

This person came to a dance we played at Poudre High School, on the west end of town. Shortly after that, we played a party at the University, and the people organizing the BOTB, told Emily, we needed to enter. Little did we know, we were again, being watched.

Talking Emma into it took all four of us.

And... in the end, we crashed and burned.

Cadi was pretty sick that night, and because she's so impossibly hardheaded, she made the decision to play anyhow – and she almost collapsed, which in turn made Emma freak out. We watched her bolt from the stage in the middle of a song.

It took us almost three months to get Emma to sing with us again, and another two, to get her in front of a crowd again. But, we eventually went back to doing what we do, and the cool part was, we were able to create some original music from all the stuff Emma had written during our 'break'.

Then, our problem started. Once Matt Duncan heard our songs, he decided we had to go, and made it his mission to bring that about.

You see, he was pissed off about the BOTB, and the fact no one wanted to hear the kind of music his band played. He decided it wasn't fair, and went on a mission to screw with as many of the bands that played that day, as he could. The idiot even managed to get himself beat up by some college guys, who were in one of the bands.

Anyhow, on a fairly quiet Saturday night, he, Nick, Ricky, and Raul, were playing at Papa Roni's. When no one applauded after they played, he got mad. Then the doofus made the mistake of getting mouthy with Lou, and that was it. On his way out, he stopped at the counter, looked right at Emma, and as he held out the mic in his hand, he said, "Hey Little Miss Nerves, you like to sing that silly pop crap, why don't you go up there and belt one out for these people..."

Lou grabbed him by the neck, and much to the surprise of everyone, Emma stopped him.

"Let him go, Papa."

The entire restaurant – which was easily two-thirds full – went totally silent, as Emma reached out, took the mic from him with one hand, and took hold of his hand with the other.

"Okay... I will. But... your rude, obnoxious self, *will* sit onstage with me until I'm done, Matthew Duncan."

You could hear a pin drop in there, I swear. Even Matt was stunned to silence – which was a first for sure.

Emma turned on the mic, and looking Matt right in the eyes, started singing *Being Noticed – without music.* Then she turned, and pulling Matt along behind her, made her way through the tables, toward the stage, singing the entire way. Strangely enough, Matt willingly followed her.

They didn't get halfway, before *everyone* in the place was clapping along. When Willie and I started toward the stage to give her some music, she shook her head, telling us not to. When she reached the stage, she turned around, sat down on the edge of it, pulled Matt down next to her, and finished the song.

And damned if Matt Duncan didn't sit motionless, and silent, holding Emma's hand, the entire time. For a split second, it seemed that Emma's voice had even gotten to him.

It was beyond amazing.

On a quiet Saturday night, in a pizza parlor, in Fort Collins, Emma Greene broke free of her demons, and in a strange way, had Matt Duncan to thank for it. She never again had a problem with being onstage, or in front of an audience.

And... although they weren't really 'friends', Emma never again, had a problem with Matt.

So... the tour.

Terri Maxwell.

Remember that name.

She's the 'mastermind'...

As fate would have it, she was in Papa Roni's the night Emma broke free. Once she heard Emma sing, we were on our way – even if we didn't know it.

The next day, we all got the same text message from Lou. *'You need to be at the restaurant at 4:00. DO NOT be late.'*

Once we discovered who she was, we pretty much freaked. Mrs. Maxwell had just one thing to say...

"I wanted to make you guys famous, but the truth is, you don't need me for that. I have no doubt you could do it on your own, with little or no effort. But, if you're interested, I would *love* to produce your first record."

Buckle your seatbelts...

fifteen

the missing piece

Emily Tao

We've been in Fort Collins for a week, and I know that soon, we'll have to go back to our real lives – such that they are. My parents asked me to stay with them, but understand my need to stay with Emma.

Every day I go on a trek around town, in an effort to work out the kinks every muscle in my body seems to have. A couple of times Willie – who is staying with his mom – turns up to walk with me. We mostly talk about business – along with being the world's best drummer, the guy is an administrative genius, – and how we'll reschedule all the appointments we cancelled. He tells me that his mom expects me to make at least a limited appearance before we leave. I suggest dinner, to which she agrees. The interesting thing is, not once does Willie press me about Emma – or what might be going on between us.

Truth is, there's nothing to tell. Although she welcomed me, and seems comfortable having me here, we don't talk much. The few conversations we have had, tell me something is still gnawing at her – from inside. Question is... what?

I'm telling Emma about the big dinner Willie's mom is having, and that everyone – parents and siblings included – has agreed to come, when there's a knock at the door. In the five days I've been here, no one has come over – period. Now, it seems we have a visitor, and seeing the visible discomfort on Emma's face, I stand up and head for the door.

"I'll see who it is. Do you want me to get rid of them?" I ask, as I reach for the handle.

Emma never responds to my question, and five seconds later, I wouldn't have heard her if she did. When I open the door, there in front of me, stands none other than Catrin Meredith – original bassist for *Audio Distortion*.

For the first time in her life, Emily Táo, almost faints.

"Hi! I was in the neighborhood and thought I'd pop in for a visit. I'm not intruding, am I?" Cadi blurts out, in her oddly British, but totally Welsh accent. When I think back to how much trouble the four of us had understanding her when we first met, it makes me smile.

The moment she breaks eye contact with me, and shifts her gaze over my shoulder, I know. I step out of the way and watch as Cadi comes in the door, and without a word, walks over to Emma, and simply wraps her arms around her. Eventually I hear sobs – from both of them. Finally, Cadi speaks…

"I'm so sorry, Emma… sorry it has taken me a year and a half to do what should have been done right away. I wanted to come back… to talk to you… to explain. At first, my body just wouldn't support the trip, and when it could, you'd pretty much made it clear you wanted your privacy."

They break their embrace, and Emma takes a step back, but never lets go of Cadi's hands.

"Every day since we moved," Cadi continues, "I've played that song – the band's song. *Every day*. In my heart, I wondered about you... about the others... about the band. I know it's my fault..."

"No," I quickly interject, "it wasn't. It wasn't anyone's *'fault'*."

"It doesn't matter," Emma adds, tears still trickling down her cheeks, but now smiling. "Destiny has been in control of all our lives from the moment we found ourselves alone in that restaurant. It's responsible for everything that has happened right up to this moment – and for this moment as well. There are reasons, Cadi, and maybe someday we'll figure them out. You'll see..."

She lets go of her hands, wipes her face, and says, "I need a moment guys..." Then she turns and disappears through a small door I know leads to her basement. When the door clicks shut, Cadi turns to face me.

"Now *that* was totally weird."

"You have no idea, Cadi... no idea. She's spent most of the last five days down there."

"'Down there'?"

"Yeah. It's her basement. I haven't been bold enough to go look, and I didn't want to press her – especially since she seems to be... well..."

"I get it. She'll tell us when she's ready, I'm sure."

"That's what I keep hoping. So, you up for a walk? I need to do my 'doctor ordered' exercise. It will give us a chance to catch up."

She smiles, wipes the remaining tears from her face, and says, "Sure, but slowly. This heat is already killing me."

We step out onto the porch, and as I close the door, a thought occurs to me.

"Does anyone else know you're here?"

"Only your mum. She picked me up. My bags are in their guest room."

"*My mom*? She has something to do with you being here?"

Cadi laughs, and finally hugs me.

"Yes. Although my parents were never crazy about the whole 'band' thing, they stayed in touch with the other parents. Believe it or not, my mum actually watched your interview. When she heard about your accident, she told my dad that it was a sign – and that it was important that I come back right away..."

Because I'm grinning like a fool, Cadi stops talking and looks at me quizzically.

"*What*?" she finally asks.

"Nothing... I completely forgot how amazing listening to you talk can be..."

"Oh *please*..." she says, without any hint of her accent – something she spent hours practicing in a time past. "Anyhow, my mom's insistence that I come back right away, wore my father down, and he finally gave in and bought me a ticket. Even though he always appeared to be against the whole 'band' thing, I think he too, knew it was time."

"Yeah, I know what you mean. It was nothing more than a 'feeling' that made me call Donna about doing the interview. Emma's 'fate and destiny' seem to be hard at work lately."

"Do you think maybe *she* feels it as well?" Cadi asks, her accent returning.

"We can hope, Cadi... we can hope..."

We hug again, lock arms, and head off down the street, in the direction of downtown, at a reasonably slow pace. After about three blocks, I make an abrupt turn, and head in a different direction.

"Come on, Cadi, let's go have a 'bit o fun' shall we?"

"Emily Táo... what are you up to?"

"We're going to the high school – to visit a couple of old friends."

Cadi shrugs, grins, and follows me down the sidewalk. All the way there, the anticipation builds – and I can't wait to see their faces.

I'm about to give 'fate and destiny' a helping hand – not that either really needs it.

sixteen

the future

Emma Greene

I write... a lot. I have to. It's what keeps me going. I have the last two years of my life, in a laptop, and saved on CDs. I've spent endless hours in what is now *my* back yard, remembering and typing.

Destiny...

For years it's been my nemesis – controlling me in ways I've always felt unfair. Giving and taking as it saw fit, and trying to make me follow a path it laid out for me. I've spent two years fighting my destiny.

And now, in ways the others don't understand, it's once again taking control. I knew the moment I saw Cadi standing on my porch.

It's 7:00 PM when Emily answers her phone, and then tells me she's going to FCHS to meet Stanley. The look on her face tells me she's hoping I'll go with her, but when I only smile at her and nod, she grabs her backpack and disappears out the door.

Unbeknownst to Emily, I make a point of keeping up with what's going on at the high school – mostly because Stan spends most of his free time there.

Tonight, some of the kids he teaches are giving a recital for their parents, and it's supposed to be over at 8:30. I'm fairly certain that Willie and Cadi will turn up as well, and they'll probably all go out afterward. The four of them have been spending *a lot* of time together – not that I didn't expect that.

Driven by the same relentless destiny, that is again manipulating all of us, twenty minutes after Emily leaves, so do I.

Halfway to the school, I pass the place it all started – Papa Roni's. It's been over two years since I was here, and I'm not at all sure what makes me do it, but I cross the parking lot, stop right outside the door, and stand staring in the window, at the crowd of college kids filling the place, and I remember… *that night…* the night fate and destiny rearranged our lives – *all five of them…*

I remember the night *Audio Distortion* was born…

After only a few moments, my reminiscing is interrupted by a hand on my shoulder. When I spin around, I find a grinning Lou behind me. He reaches out, and wipes the tears off my cheeks.

"Good memories, I hope?"

"The only kind I will ever have about you, and this place, Papa…" I reply, hugging him.

"When are you guys coming to play here again?" he asks.

I laugh – loudly.

"Maybe sooner that you know, Papa! I gotta run. Some people are waiting for me."

He kisses my cheek, then I turn and head off in the direction of the high school, with a now strangely different attitude.

Thirty minutes later, I'm standing in the dark, listening to the music coming from the Music Hall in front of me, staring blankly at the back door. Within seconds, the tears begin…

The sound of gravel crunching jerks me right back to reality – and scares the crap out of me. I jump – and yell – as I spin around, tears still trickling down my cheeks.

"Good evening, Miss Greene. Here for the recital?"

I recognize the voice the moment I hear it.

"Mr. Ramos?"

"Who were you expecting?"

"Uh... well... *no one*? It's almost 8:00 at night."

"Got to clean the place sometime, right?" he replies, rolling his now empty trashcan over and stopping next to me.

I'm amazed that he looks exactly like he did the first time I met him – the first time Mrs. Dreesen let us use the Hall to rehearse. When I just stand staring at him, he smiles, turns, and walks over to the door I'm in front of, sticks one of his many keys into the lock and opens it.

"Go ahead... You can listen from backstage," he says, holding the door open.

"I... uhh... well..."

"Emma, you are standing in front of this particular door for a reason, not by accident. All those tears tell me you need answers only you can find. If you don't want them to know you are here, just come back out this way. I'll leave the alarm off until 11:00, when I go home."

Not knowing what else to do, and feeling a strong pull from something inside, I force a smile and go in. After about ten steps, I hear the door close behind me, and when I turn to look, find that I'm alone – Mr. Ramos doesn't follow me.

Destiny... so many things needing to happen in a specific way.

Without fully realizing what's happening, sixty seconds later, I find myself standing outside the dressing rooms, listening to the kids playing out front.

I turn the handle on the door nearest me, and finding it unlocked, push it open. It's dark inside, and after finding the switch, I turn on the lights, and let the door close. I walk over, and sit down at the make-up table, and let my mind wander...

"Would I have let them talk me into it," I ask my reflection, "if I'd known what it would eventually cost me?"

I feel the tears – one thing I am *intimately* familiar with – coming again, as I sit alone, staring at myself in the mirror.

Then a weird thing happens.

I hear music – but it isn't the recital...

When I turn and look behind me, I see them – Stanley, Cadi, Emily, and Willie – in the back of the room, playing, and realize the music is in my head. Although I know they aren't real, I get up and walk toward them.

We were five ordinary kids, who by chance and coincidence, met in a small pizza parlor. Then one night, solely in the interest of amusing ourselves, and completely by accident, we create a catchy little song about our lives and the single thing we share...

A love of music.

As I stand here, my flashback running in front of me, I hear *my* voice – and realize... *I'm singing...*

Wondering when
Their time will come
Wondering when
The world will notice

I smile, and find myself wondering how many of the kids that have *'Being Noticed'* on their mp3 players, realize it was totally ad-libbed?

Lyrics that turned out to be so powerful and meant so much to so many, were made-up on a quiet Friday night, by an overly shy, fifteen year old girl, as she watched her friends playing...

When, right in the middle of the chorus, I feel the hand on my shoulder, I almost have a heart attack – and immediately stop singing.

"Took you long enough, Emma..." I hear from a female voice behind me.

I spin around, and find myself face to face with Mrs. Dreesen, who apparently managed – *in complete silence* – to sneak in.

"How...?" I mutter, completely confused.

"Victor called me – how do you think, silly?" she replies. *"And..."* she continues, obviously fighting off a laugh, "this is the only room with a light on in it..."

She quits talking, sits down on a couch next to her, and for thirty seconds, we quietly stare at each other. I finally take a seat next to her, and wipe the tears off my face. Once I'm done, she hands me a large padded envelope she has in her hands.

"What's this?"

"Destiny, Emma. The moment Catrin collapsed in Berlin, something told me that a time would come, when I would need it," she replies, nodding at me to indicate she wants me to open it.

I lift the flap on the unsealed end and carefully pull out what turns out to be a framed photograph, of the giant banner that was hanging over the entrance of Moby Arena, the night we played our first ever real concert.

Across the bottom is some hand written text...

And though our lives
Were thrown together
No options ever ours
Our hearts and minds
Are bound together
By friendships that will last forever...

With something as simple as a faded photograph, and lyrics I'd written, Mrs. Dreesen is able to make me understand. Before I know it, I'm sobbing, and gently rubbing the glass covering the photo, hoping beyond hope, that I'll be able to do, what I know I need to do.

"The path each of us must follow on the way to fulfilling our individual destiny is very seldom smooth or uncomplicated. Yours, Emma, is far more complicated than the others, because it is, and always has been, part of *the band's* destiny."

As we sit quietly, I find myself unable to pull my eyes away from the photograph. She waits for a bit, and then Mrs. Dreesen breaks the silence with her final comment.

"*Emma Greene* is – and will always be – the lead singer for *Audio Distortion*. They're waiting on you – the band, *and* your fans. Emily said it perfectly on TV – '*when you are ready*' – and the four of them believe that, in their hearts."

With a smile, she stands up, kisses me on the forehead, then turns and goes out the door, as I sit crying, and staring at the photo.

Ten minutes later, now scared to death, I wander into the hall and up the back stage stairs. I hear voices... but no music. I figure the recital is over, and that my friends are probably straightening things up before they leave. I pull open part of the side curtain, and when I peek into the Hall, I see a few kids helping Mrs. Dreesen and Stan put things away on the stage, while six or seven parents wait patiently for them to finish.

Willie and Cadi are sitting in the front row talking to each other, and Emily is standing near the stairs, talking to a kid who is holding a guitar case. I stand quietly for a few seconds, and watch – and enjoy the sensation of seeing the four of them *together* again…

Then, I hear the kid Emily is talking to ask if she's really the lead guitarist for *Audio Distortion*, and pretty much know what's going to happen next.

I also know it is *way* past time… for them… *for all of us* actually.

I hear Willie laugh, as he stands up, pulls a pair of drumsticks out of his back pocket (some things never change), and gently jabs the kid in the ribs with one.

"I'm the drummer!" he says to the kid, and starts a beat with his sticks.

I couldn't stop the huge smile that spreads across my face, even if I wanted to. At this point, they have the undivided attention of *all* the kids – as well as a few of the parents.

Cadi – now also grinning – follows Willie up the stairs and, two steps short of the top, turns and looks at the same kid.

"You want us to prove it?" she asks, looking him right in the eyes.

One of the kids makes a comment about Cadi's accent, and her mother playfully cuts her off by putting both hands over her mouth.

Emily, now laughing, also climbs the stairs and follows the others onto the stage, as the remaining kids and parents crowd up to the edge and stand watching.

Mrs. Dreesen lets out a laugh, and yells, "*Finally!*"

Still, no one has noticed my presence. I let go of the curtain, turn and go back the way I came, ending up in the backstage hall again.

Within seconds, they're well into the opening of *Being Noticed* as they laugh and joke among themselves. It is apparent Cadi is out of practice as, just before they reach the first stanza, she misses some chords, lets out a laugh, and they all start picking on her. The kids immediately egg them on to try again, which of course they do.

Having followed the hall, I'm now standing in front of the door that will let me out into the Hall, right next to the stage stairs. Time for Emma to do what needs to be done...

When they make it through the intro a second time, I push the door open, and without any warning, I open my mouth and just start singing. The acoustics in the Hall are such that I don't need a microphone...

On a quiet night
I was cleaning tables

The moment they hear me, every single head turns my direction, the kids all get excited, and their parents start clapping...

Watching the band
Knowing they're able

I start toward the stairs, and for the first time in over two years, *I sing an Audio Distortion song...*

Wondering when
Their time will come

I totally let my voice – *and my heart* – go, and the result is full on, *lead singer*, vocals – the way the song is meant to be performed. The way we've performed it hundreds of times...

Wondering when
Someone will notice

My heart is racing, the tears again begin to fall – but it feels *AWESOME*…

Emily and Cadi – both in a bit of shock – never miss a beat, and fall in on backup vocals at the first chorus…

We're here!
Night after night
We're here!
Under the lights
Hoping we'll get noticed…

When I reach the stairs, I glance at Mrs. Dreesen, and see that she too, has tears in her eyes. I raise my eyebrows, hold up the photograph, and keep right on singing…

Fifteen minutes later, standing backstage, I tell the four of them I need to be alone again for a bit. Being the awesome friends they are, they each nod their understanding, hug me, and go back out to put the instruments away. Mrs. Dreesen is last…

"Thank you…" I say, holding out the photo to her.

"You should keep it…" she says, before I interrupt her.

"No… *you* should. That way, no matter where I am, I will always know where it is…" I quickly say, smiling and closing her hand around the frame, "…in case I need another 'nudge'."

I hug her, kiss her on the cheek, and then slip out the back door.

Usually, being out in public (I have a weird fear of being recognized) makes me nervous, and I'm always in a rush to get home.

Not tonight.

The freeing sensation of what happened at the school, has completely engulfed me, and tonight, I just wander around aimlessly… for more than two hours. I even force myself to stay on the main streets – around *people*...

Everyone I pass smiles, and says things like 'Hi' and 'nice night', and twice, while standing on corners, I even get whistles from passing cars. If anyone *did* recognize me, not a single one let on...

I find myself wondering why I let myself slip so far...

I finally make it home around midnight, and find Emily sound asleep on the couch, with the TV on, and the sound muted. I think she was waiting up for me.

Smiling, I pull a light blanket up over her, turn everything off and go to bed.

seventeen

direction

Emma Greene

When I got up this morning, Emily was nowhere to be found, but the blanket was neatly folded, and lying on the couch. On top of it was a note saying she'd gone to her parents' and would be back later – and if I needed her, to call her cell. At the very bottom was a cute little smilie face, and the words 'WHEN YOU ARE READY' in prefect little block letters.

It made me smile.

It takes just more than hour – and three cups of coffee – before I'm fully awake and able to sort out the jumble of confused emotions, caused by the previous evening's antics.

I get my laptop, my portable Yamaha keyboard, and head for the backyard – the place I do my best writing.

Based on one quick online search, it's apparent that Emily's interview has already stirred things up again. Within hours, Stan received no less than six phone calls from news agencies, and Willie mentioned that at least three had left messages at the studio. Realizing that most of the music world will now be looking for explanations, I figure I'll just write out my part of it. Once I'm done, they can do with it what they see fit.

This is what I have so far…

No, contrary to what seems to be popular belief, I'm not crazy.

Yes, like millions of other people around the world, I have issues.

Based on the first eighteen years of my life, my issues may go a bit deeper than most other people's.

Losing my dad was… well… hard – but not in the way you think. Although the formation of Audio Distortion, and the friendships that have come from it, prompted me to try to renew my relationship with him, we simply didn't have enough time. I still have his photo – a really old one – and sometimes I can hear his voice, or what I remember his voice to be, but we were nonetheless, still very much strangers to each other. Everything else aside, I will never forget, he was my dad.

Losing Grams was different. Grams was all I had in the world. I know that losing Dad, is what killed her. Because she spent so much time, dreaming about, and planning for, the day he would recover, the realization that it wasn't ever going to happen, was more than her very old heart could take.

Maybe… it was God's way of getting them together again.

Anyhow, the moment I saw Cadi standing on my porch, I realized that it was time. Her presence told me something was about to change – again. I knew that fate and destiny were sending me a message.

Audio Distortion — Replay

Back on tour, losing Cadi had been the beginning of my 'slide into oblivion'. First, Dad's accident, then three weeks later Cadi gets sick. From the moment she collapsed on that stage in Berlin, a deep seeded fear took hold of my heart – the fear that her medical conditions would take her away from us forever.

I knew there was no way I could take another person close to me dying.

Then, in Madrid, they told me about Grams.

Yes, I lost it. Completely. I'm not sure if I was more terrified, or angry.

So, without any warning, to anyone, I ran home and have been hiding ever since. As long as I stayed isolated in my little world, there wouldn't be anyone to lose – that's what I spent day after day trying to convince myself of. And, although I dearly love Stan, I pushed him away too. I had to.

I've spent the last year of my life reading, and writing, and trying desperately to understand why… why destiny has chosen to complicate my life the way it has.

Yes, I have a voice – one that many say is a gift. Yes, I have a way with words and can, through verse, communicate almost anything. I often wonder if having these things – these 'gifts' – is a tradeoff.

In order to get, I have to give – almost everything.

And now, the part of my life that for whatever reason, destiny has so diligently orchestrated, is back.

I never wanted to be famous – I swear. I like reading, and more so, writing. I'd be content to

publish a book of poetry, or spend my days writing songs that others can sing.
Thanks Stan...
Yeah, that's right. I went through all this for Stanley. Since the day I first laid eyes on the guy, I've had the biggest crush on him.
Unfortunately, I couldn't find a way to tell him. Well... until the VH1 interview – when I opened my mouth to cover Cadi. The moment he took my hand, we knew.
Now I sit here, ready to once again find my way. My heart is telling me that my new path will include the four of them, and hopefully, my 'family' is ready...

Knowing that music is my best motivation, I power up the keyboard, plug it into the laptop, and launch my editing program. I find the song (easily my favorite) I want, click play, and the first few chords send me right to the place I need to be...

I close my eyes, and remember the first time I heard them. Then an image forms...

Cadi – frustrated and headed toward the door in a huff. Willie – arms crossed on his snare, and his head resting on them. And of course Emily – gently banging her head on the wall, her guitar still around her shoulders, looking as frustrated and depressed as a person can.

Then... Stanley saved us. With just nine notes, he saved *Audio Distortion*. In a matter of seconds – the time it takes a heart to beat three or four times – we went from being five individuals, to being a *band*...

Stan's intro started the machine, but the moment I heard Willie jump in on his drums, the rhythm he created pushed a button in me, and I knew I had the perfect lyrics – words quickly scrawled in a notebook, as I sat eating my lunch on a sunny afternoon.

All I needed to make it work was for *all four of them* to come together, for just a couple of minutes, and give me the music...

That day in the music room at FCHS – our first real 'rehearsal' – was the day I stepped up and became a 'frontman'. It was the day I truly began to believe that *we could be a band*...

The song is in the second stanza before I realize I'm once again singing – which makes me smile. I reach down, reset the song, and after some careful manipulation, remove the track that contains the lead vocals. I hit play again, and for the second time in as many days, I sing an *Audio Distortion* song – and give it everything I have...

eighteen

intervention

Emma Greene

I'm so caught up in what I'm doing, I never hear them. Somehow, they manage to sneak in through my back gate. My concentration is broken by Cadi's giggling. Halfway through the last stanza, I stop, spin around on the grass, and am met by twenty smiling faces, and a loud round of applause, and whistling.

Without a word, Stan steps over and holds out his hand to me.

This is the next pivotal moment in my life. In that instant I decide I'm finished hiding... finished avoiding. I reach over, close the laptop, power down the keyboard, and then take his hand. He pulls me to my feet, and with the crowd of onlookers watching, puts a microphone in my hand. I stand for a moment, contemplating what it means. As I close my hand around it, I realize it feels... well... *right*. It's meant to be there...

I feel myself smile, and when I look up, I see that my band mates all have the exact same mic in their hands, and some seriously sinister smiles on their faces.

"Come on, Emma, we have a small task to take care of," Emily says, taking my free hand and leading me in the direction of the gate, causing the crowd to part enough for us to get through, "and it's going to take all five of us to do it."

"And 'no' isn't an option this time," I hear Cadi say behind me, in her usual hard to understand Welsh accent.

We pile into Willie's BMW, and watch as he closes and locks the gate, before getting in behind the wheel. At the end of the alley, as Willie turns onto the pavement, I glance over my shoulder and out the back window.

"And who were they?" I ask, pointing at the now dispersing crowd.

"*Fans*," Emily replies, laughing. "Heck, *we* heard you when we made the turn into the alley."

"They were crowded around the gate and I had to push my way through them to unlock it," Stan offers, also laughing.

"Like it or not," Cadi adds, "when *you* sing, people notice."

No one says anything else the rest of the trip. I do notice that Stanley never once lets go of my hand.

The sun is dropping behind the mountains, as we pull into the packed parking lot of Moby Arena – CSU'S basketball arena – at the southern end of campus, twenty minutes later. Stanley, sensing my nervousness, leans over and whispers in my ear.

"Relax. You're going to get a kick out of this... trust me."

When Security stops us, Willie hands him a card, and with a smile, he waves us through. As we pull into what is undoubtedly a reserved spot, I see the huge sign hanging over the arena entrance. Even though I have no idea what's going on, it makes me laugh.

The moment Cadi opens her door, and I hear the music... my heart races. It's been a long time...

Standing in a tight circle next to the SUV, we watch as people hurriedly pass us, heading for the arena entrance. I find it interesting that none of them seems to recognize us – or perhaps, it's that their attention is on the live music being played inside.

"Okay," Stan says, pulling his mic from his pocket and holding it up "these are on the same frequency as the ones our arch nemeses are using. You guys remember a certain night at the Battle of the Bands, right?"

We – me included – break up in almost hysterical laughter, loud enough that at least a few of the passing *Always Louder* fans, slow to look at us.

"Tonight, my fellow disruptors, we exact some revenge."

"Stanley Campbell!" I blurt out, desperately trying not to laugh again. "We *are not* going to go in there and purposely mess up their show."

Again, everyone laughs, and I realized at this very moment, that for the first time since my grandmother died, I truly feel like *me* again. I am, for a few seconds, *Emma Greene – frontman for Audio Distortion*.

"Yeah... maybe not. But they *are* going to know, we came to their show!" Stan retorts.

He spends fifteen minutes explaining the plan, making sure we understand. Fifteen minutes after that, having entered the building separately, we're all in position, mingling with the crowd, within feet of the stage.

What I don't know, that everyone else does, is that Matt Duncan, as well as all the other members of *Always Louder,* are willingly participating in what's about to happen.

nineteen

emily's plan

Emily Tao

My intention is to let the world see us all together again. Once we're discovered in the crowd, Matt and Nick ask us up on stage, we apologize for messing with their performance, and joke about it being retribution for the relentless taunting we endured at the hands of Matt, when we crashed and burned at the Battle of the Bands, years ago. Then we quietly disappear, and let them continue their show.

Thanks to Matt and Nick, my plan works far better than I ever imagined. Tonight at Moby Arena, will prove to be the second pivotal moment in *Audio Distortion*'s history. With one simple gesture, Matt Duncan – the guy who did everything he could to destroy us, a few years earlier – brings us back.

Apparently, and unbeknownst to me, Matt and Nick have a completely different idea of how things are going to go. And to be honest with you, I'm in awe of them for coming up with it.

As a group, *Always Louder* has changed – both their style and lyrics. The bizarre, obnoxious, 'headbangers' who went out of their way to mess with us at the Battle of the Bands, and despised our existence, have given way to a really good rock band that sings about the trials and tribulations of everyday life.

When Nick and Cadi, became a 'couple' (yeah... like the world didn't expect that?), Nick ended up traveling – and on occasion, playing – with us on our tour. When *Always Louder* reformed, Nick drew from his experiences while with us, to write a couple of touching ballads, as well as a few slightly less annoying, semi-brain-mangling songs. While not the typical *Always Louder* songs, Matt puts his heart and soul into each one, and delivers them flawlessly. No matter what one says about Matt Duncan, the one undeniable fact is, the guy can sing, and fortunately, for the world of music, he's learned the art of compromise. The four of them have developed a pretty dedicated following.

I'm standing at the far right of the stage, and staggered at distances of a few feet are Willie, Emma, Stan, and Cadi. By design, Emma ends up center-stage. The guys finish their first song, and as Matt is about to announce the next one, Nick interrupts him.

"One sec, Matt... I have a question for the audience," Nick says, as Matt hands him the mic. "So people, for about a week now, I've had a weird urge to play some of our old stuff – the stuff we did back in high school. Some of you might remember it..."

The crowd starts cheering and whistling.

"Would you guys have a problem with that?"

This time, the place totally erupts in screams, whistles, and stomping.

Matt laughs, Nick yells "*OH YEAH!*" into the mic, and then tosses it back to Matt, who immediately points at Raul, the bass player. Instantly the entire arena goes dark and within seconds, is filled with the opening chords of their *original title song*...

My pulse rate doubles.

First, Matt's booming voice fills the darkness...

Glad you made it to the show
Time for us to totally let go

Then, a single spotlight pierces the darkness and illuminates Matt, as he continues the song...

Livin' large, makin' noise
You know you want,
To play with our toys

Before you know it, the place is aglow with the light of a thousand green glow-sticks, bobbing in perfect unison to the beat...

Makin' music's our forte
Bangin' heads, every day

When Matt reaches the chorus, the five of us turn on our mics, and much to the surprise of the fans around us, make our presence known. When the lights come up on the stage, and Matt sings...

Wind us up, watch us go
We want the world to know

...the rest of the band joins him on the last line of the chorus...

We are... Always Louder!

...and right on cue, five amplified voices cover it...

We are... Always Louder!

...and it is *so insanely loud*, you can *feel* it! Apparently, all five of our mics are feeding the same amp. The crowd goes totally off, the very second it happens.

Feigning a look of shock and disbelief, then looking at Nick and raising his hands as of if to say 'what's going on', Matt never misses a beat and finishes the chorus with his own...

Why yes we are...

Matt continues into the next verse, Nick and Raul move to the edge of the stage and stand there, as if looking for something... *or someone.* When Matt reaches the chorus the second time, he gets the same response – with one small change. Having been discovered by the crowd, both Emma – who is now laughing like a fool – and Cadi, have enlisted the help of the fans around them, and with twenty or so people all singing the chorus together, the amplified sound is almost deafening.

When Matt starts the last verse, Emma puts a finger to her lips, and astonishingly, *everyone* around her goes silent, and lets Matt – who is now at the very edge of the stage, only feet from her – finish the song.

When they reach the final chorus, Matt holds out his mic to indicate they want the crowd to sing, and once they sing...

We are... **Always Louder!**

...the final time, Matt counts 'four-three-two-one' and not only do all the lights go out, but amazingly, *every single glow-stick stops moving, at the exact same moment*, as Matt's voice is heard throughout the now-dark, yet eerily green-glowing building...

Why yes... yes we are...

...which is followed by a very weird, echoed silence, which seems to last forever.

The eruption of insanity that follows simply can't be described with words...

I'm standing in the darkness, with goose bumps covering most of my body, and through all the cheering, screaming, whistling, and stomping that starts around me, I hear only one thing...

Emma Greene... *laughing hysterically.*

twenty

matt's plan

Stanley Campbell

When Emily told us what she'd done, we were ecstatic – even Cadi. It's time – and we know it. We just need to convince Emma of that.

While Nick and Matt showing up at my house, the morning of their show, isn't a big deal, what they want is close to 'off the chart weird' – more so, because it's actually *Matt's* idea.

As Emma likes to say – *fate and destiny*.

Anyhow, they agree that getting the five of us on stage together will definitely be a step in the right direction, but Matt *insists* we need to perform – at least one song.

Standing in my kitchen, only inches from me, Matt locks eyes with me…

"If you guys get up there, and then walk off without getting her to sing, it will be the dumbest thing you have ever done as a group – and you know it, Stan."

The deep, and total sincerity in his voice, reaches all the way to my core.

"When Emily came to you guys, it wasn't about messing up or hijacking…"

"Stan, that's crap, and you know it," Nick interjects. "This is about way more than 'our show'. This is about Emma. *All of you, in the same place at the same time?*"

He pauses, and holds my gaze for a few seconds.

"*Come on man* – you have to go for this, there just isn't any other choice…"

I stand watching the two of them bang fists and wink at each other, definitely a bit perplexed. Although I have no idea what they're up to, I know it isn't in any way devious or obnoxious. Their concern for Emma is indeed, sincere.

"Okay… so I can tell you two have some kind of plan. What do I need to do?"

"We don't have keyboards," Matt says, "so give us your Roland AX, we'll make sure it's amped, and stash it on stage. Once we get all of you up there, Raul will tell you where it is, and while I'm busy annoying Emma…"

Nick and I both laugh at his comment.

"…you can set up," he continues. "Willie, Emily and Cadi can use our gear."

"We'll give you guys the stage," Nick adds, putting a hand on my shoulder, "and no matter what, Stanley, *you've got to get her to sing*… at least one song. If she leaves that stage without singing… well…"

I knew exactly what he meant.

Now, eight hours later, here I am, standing in front of the stage, watching Emma in a crowd of *Always Louder* fans, laughing hysterically – something I honestly wondered if I would ever see again – and getting high-fived repeatedly! The sound of the cheering crowd is finally broken by the amplified voice of Matt Duncan…

"YO-YO, *Louder* fans! I think I've discovered the source of our unexpected backup singers – right here in front of the stage. And thanks to all of you! I don't think I've ever heard that song performed quite like that before. *You guys totally freakin' rock!*"

Then we hear Nick's voice, and as I stand here watching, it dawns on me that, what once were our two biggest problems, have now become our saviors.

"You two," Nick says, with total force and conviction while pointing at Cadi with one hand, and Emma with the other, "need to come up here right now." The moment he points, spotlights go right to the girls.

"And, considering we *all* grew up here, I'm betting the other three culprits are out there somewhere too!" Matt adds.

Even as Matt is talking, more spots start scanning the crowd, and according to Emily's plan, we all start moving toward center stage. The moment I'm close enough, although she's still smiling, I can see the panic and fear covering Emma's face. She looks just like she did when we found her in the storage room at Papa Roni's.

"Well?" Matt says, as we all converge at the stairs leading to the stage.

The five of us stand motionless – four staring at Emma and her staring back at us.

Then we hear Nick's voice boom out.

"I can't believe that the infamous *Audio Distortion* is afraid of a little stage time! Yep, that's right – they're here people. The five *original* members of *Audio Distortion* are standing right there, at the bottom of the stairs."

Nick Sharpe is a genius. Having spent six months on tour with *Audio Distortion*, he carefully watched and noted each time a manager, technician, or roadie, would do something that would push one of Emma's buttons. Even though she once told me 'perfection is way over rated', when it came to our live shows, she always demanded it. And now, Nick's attention has paid off – big time. Of the many buttons Emma seems to have, he just picked the perfect one to push. The moment her facial expression changes – the fear and panic being replaced by the controlled irritation we saw many a time on tour – we realize that Emily's plan is about to become reality.

Emma hands her mic to me, turns, and pretty much stomps up onto the stage, continuing across it until she is face to face with Matt. Without as much as a word to him, she takes the mic he's holding, turns it on, and with the most devious sneer I have ever seen on the girl, looks him in the eyes, and very calmly says, "Hello, *Matthew*..."

Immediately the crowd is full of whistles, sneers, and jeers. With just two words, Emma pulls the crowd into what's about to happen.

Then she turns, walks directly over to Nick, and with the mic still powered, lets him have it... playfully of course.

"Nick Sharpe, I am shocked! *You of all people* should realize that, while *we* may not have a lot of recent 'stage time', the very last thing that *Audio Distortion* would be afraid of, would be sharing a stage with *Always Louder*..."

Yeah... Nick blushes... *bright red!* And again, the crowd goes completely off...

It's by far, the most magical thing I've ever seen. Just like two years ago, in a pizza parlor, in a single instant, Emma Greene emerges from whatever has been gripping her for the last year, and in front of 5000 people, just as she did so many times on tour, takes control of a stage. It may be *Always Louder's* show, but at this exact moment, *the stage belongs to Emma Greene* – without question. And... as weird as it is, like last time, Matt Duncan is involved.

The applause, screaming, whistling, and stomping that follow Emma's comment, makes it feel as if the building shakes. Even the bands that opened the show come out to see what's going on.

We start up the stairs – totally stunned by Emma's response to the situation – as she turns off the mic, stands on her tiptoes and in front of the entire arena, kisses Nick on the cheek. She whispers to him, he nods and hugs her, and then she turns around, walks back across the stage to Matt, stops facing him, and hands him the mic.

"Okay... okay..." Matt says, trying to bring the sound level in the building down, so that he can be heard. "You are seeing the *original members* of *Audio Distortion*, on a stage together, for the first time in... well... let's just call it forever, shall we?"

Then he turns to Emma, and as we stop behind her, asks, "So... want to tell us why?"

Emma glances at us, grins, then again takes Matt's mic and says, "Retribution, Matt. You *must* remember The Battle of the Bands..." as calmly as you please.

We do our best not to laugh... but... well, it doesn't work out. Once Cadi starts giggling, Emily follows, and in seconds we're all – the crowd included – full on laughing, as Emma holds out the mic, and Matt takes it back.

"Yeah, well, I do still owe you an apology for that one. Better late, than never, right?"

This time, instead of taking the mic, Emma, who's on the verge of laughter herself, pulls Matt's hand over, mic and all.

"Apology accepted. We're even now."

More applause and whistling.

As Matt turns to face the crowd, I step back, hoping Emma won't notice, and go get the Roland.

"So… as long as we have them here," Matt says, as the lighting guys bring up the house lights, and start scanning the crowd with spots again – in an effort to hold Emma's attention, "should we get them to play? At least one song…?"

Once again, the place erupts.

Matt turns back to face the others, and although looking right at Emma, he asks all of them, "You guys up to that?"

Emily who, along with Cadi and Willie, isn't expecting this, flips on the mic she's still holding, and in almost a whisper, says, "You'll have to ask our lead singer…"

It gets so eerily quiet, you'd think the place was empty.

Then, through the momentary silence, those of us onstage, hear someone softly crying. Matt, being one step ahead of the rest of us, realizes that it's Emma, and he does what very well might be the coolest thing he's ever done. With a big grin, he steps right up to her, and as the silent crowd watches, switches off his mic, puts it in her hand, and carefully closes her fingers around it. Then, as if we're all once again standing around in Papa Roni's, everyone on stage hears him say, in just above a whisper, *"Hey, Little Miss Nerves, you like to sing that silly pop crap, why don't you belt one out for these people…"*

After hesitating for only a second, Emma, with tears trickling down her cheeks, puts a hand on his cheek, and kisses him too – smack on the lips! The instant it happens, I know…

I adjust the keyboard, and when I nod at Raul, he signals someone, the lights go out again, and I start playing. Even though the Roland has lighted keys, I don't need to see... I know the chords by heart, and simply let my heart control my fingers. It takes three times through the intro, during which time, the others get ready, but eventually, Emma's smooth, powerful, and amazingly perfect voice, fills the dark arena.

When times are tough
When hearts are broken
When things are at their worst

A single spotlight comes on – directly on Emma, who is now sitting alone at the top of the stairs we came up, circled by a bunch of fans. In seconds, the place is again glowing green with *hundreds* of light sticks, slowly moving from side to side...

Friendship first
Music follows
On this crazy road we travel

The lights go out again, and the moment Emily strikes the first chord on Nick's guitar... after well over a year and a half, and all the discouraging things we've endured as band, and as individuals, we are once again – *in this exact moment* – those five kids from the pizza parlor...

We are Audio Distortion.

And let me tell you... Emma's performance leaves no doubt we are back.

twenty-one

recovery

Emma Greene

We play just that one song – our 'signature' song. It makes me remember how awesome performing in front of a real audience feels, *and* how much I miss it.

Having quickly escaped the building, the five of us are standing in the parking lot next to Willie's SUV, listening as *Always Louder* finishes their set. The four pairs of eyes, silently staring at me, tell me they all have the same question burning behind them. But, being the awesome friends they are, not one of them asks. Stanley, however, has a comment...

"So..." he says, breaking the silence, "apparently you *have* been exercising those vocal chords..."

Everyone – including me – instantly breaks out in laughter, as I step over and wrap my arms around him. We break the embrace, and I turn to the others.

"Thank you – *all of you*."

They take turns hugging me, and when they're finished, I turn and give Stanley a kiss.

"I'm gonna walk home guys..."

It takes me close to three minutes and a good bit of insistence, to convince my friends that I'll be okay walking home. I tell them I need to slow down and let my brain catch up with my heart, and that I need to be alone to do it. Cadi asks if she can come with me, but we can see that just the one performance, has taken a lot out of her, so I tell her no. Emily saves me by quickly suggesting they take Cadi to her parents' house, so she can rest and wind down too, and the guys instantly agree. After some quick goodbyes, with a big smile, I head off across the campus.

When Matt, with what I am sure were tears in his eyes, stepped up to me on that stage, handed me his mic, and said, *"Hey Little Miss Nerves..."* I knew destiny was slapping me in the face, and was using Matt to do it.

I flashed back to a pizzeria... what seemed like forever ago... and remembered *that* Emma.

In that single moment of time – while Matt and I were staring at each other, every one of the walls I surrounded myself with for over a year, simply collapsed – just like that night at Papa Roni's. And, like the last time, Matt Duncan is responsible. How weird is that? Now... it seems I owe Matt a debt of sorts. His antics made me realize that I'm more than ready to be onstage again. The moment the lights went out and I heard Stan's keyboard, I was *ready to sing again.*

More importantly, I actually *wanted to.*

It will take me about an hour to walk the two and a half miles home, which is cool. I'm in no hurry, and the truth is, I need to be alone after that rush of intensity.

The amazingly good mood I'm in bursts out when I see the bench at the bus stop. For no particular reason, the moment I'm close enough, I jump up on it and, without care one to who might be watching, jump up and down three times, and do 'the slide' – the silly thing we do when we play *Crazy Road* – across it, giggling the whole time. At the opposite end, I jump off, and continue my journey.

Once it started, I was pretty sure the whole 'performance' thing was a set up for my benefit, but had no idea how deep it went until, in the shadowy darkness of the stage, I saw Nick *give* Emily his guitar, and Raul, with a huge grin on his face, give his bass to Cadi. I turned around, tears still trickling down my face, just in time to see Stan, his Roland strung around his neck, start the intro. The whole thing was important to the point that, the members of *both bands*, were willing to put themselves on the spot, in front of an arena full of people, with nothing but the *hope* I would sing…

They are *all* amazing to a point that only my heart can understand.

Even as Stanley started the intro, I crossed the stage, and sat down on the stairs, contemplating what was about to happen, realizing that *yes,* I actually *wanted* it to. I purposely waited until the others were ready before I started singing. It was strange hearing my amplified voice again, as I sang the intro – six lines that once again, carried so much meaning.

I wait for the light at the next intersection, and as I cross the street, I stop – for no particular reason – and start waving at people sitting in their cars at the light. Once I have them all waving and laughing, I continue across, and on the other side, turn and head the direction I need to go – still laughing like a fool.

Back at the show, my recovery was complete the instant Emily struck the first chords on Nick's guitar, and by the time I reached the first chorus, she, Cadi, and I, were jumping up and down and doing our infamous 'slide' – for like the millionth time. By the second chorus, the three of us synced up, and in a matter of seconds, *everyone* within thirty feet of the stage was jumping and sliding in almost perfect unison with us.

It was *a w e s o m e!*

And... I was crying the entire time.

At the next intersection, I grab the street sign, and walk around it three times, going on and off the curb each time. A group of college students waiting to cross on the opposite side, break out laughing, and begin egging me on. Once I'm done entertaining them, I make a left and head down the street I know will take me home.

At the beginning of the next block, still consumed by an amazing 'freeing' feeling, I go to the edge of the sidewalk, and start walking down the curb with one foot, and in the gutter with the other. Some kids, getting out of their mother's car in their driveway, see me, and after they crack up laughing, run down and begin following my silly antics – all the way to the next corner. Finally, when their mother calls them back, they all wave at me and yell goodbye. I cross the street and continue toward the house.

In the middle of the next block – which is where my house is – I turn down the alley. Because it sounds like a good idea at the moment, and totally fits my mood, I start walking backwards, and singing *We Are*. Just short of the gate into my backyard, I hear a male voice – which I recognize – yell at me from a second floor window, of the house next door.

"Maybe they're right, Emma – maybe you ARE crazy!" the voice calls out, immediately following the comment with laughter.

"Of course they are, Mr. Warner – of course they are!" I yell back.

"It's wonderful to hear you singing again young lady!" he retorts, as I reach the gate.

I wave and watch as he closes his window, then pull out my keys, and unlock gate. As I cross the back yard, I pick up the laptop and the keyboard, and head for the basement.

At the bottom of the stairs, I flip on the lights, and as I walk across the room, I touch each piece of equipment as I pass it.

A Yamaha DGX 230 keyboard – just like Stan's, an old Spring Hill acoustic guitar that I learned on, a beautiful Ibanez AC240 that the band gave me on my birthday, and my grandmother's very old Monarch Upright Piano that I had restored, so I could use it.

Once I have the Yamaha safely in its case, I sit down at the computer I've spent the better part of the last year in front of – writing – and as I stare at it, I smile. I turn and roll the few feet to the large book case, and pull out one of the twenty-five or so, three inch binders filling it, and just flip it open. I read what's on the page, and immediately remember writing it.

I saved it all – every single lyric I've written in the last fourteen months, and most of the music as well. I'm not sure why, but something kept telling me I was going to need it all.

"When I show them the basement, I'll bet they freak," I mumble to Jasper, when she jumps up into my lap.

I plug the charger into the laptop, then open it, and save what I was working on earlier. Once it powers down, I pick up Jasper and go back upstairs, turning the lights off as I leave.

It's been an exhausting day – the first one I've had in forever – and it feels really good. I stop at the stairs, and look at a photo of me and Grams that's hanging on the wall, and with a smile say, "I think I've finally found my way, Grams..."

I'm asleep within minutes of hitting my bed.

twenty-two

being ready

Emily Tao

We meet for breakfast the next morning – Stan, Willie, Cadi and me. We're wound tight – performing together again, pumped us up. Fact is, we want more – even Cadi – who struggled through all the dancing.

But the reality of it is, without our frontman, *Audio Distortion* will never be again. We all agree on that. None of us is interested in *Audio Distortion* with a new singer, and starting a new band isn't a consideration for any of us.

None of us want to press Emma. Heck, we saw how last night affected her. It took everything she had, to pull off such a monster spur-of-the-moment performance, and for now, that's enough for us.

So... if Emma isn't ready, the world will have to wait until she is – no matter how long that takes.

But... we can keep hoping.

Just about the time we finish eating, Janet – a girl from Stan and Willie's days at Fort Collins High – rushes up to the table, almost out of breath. In her hands is a Sony S1 tablet, with a video running on it.

"*You guys have got to see this!*" she yells, handing me the device, which I lean up against the napkin holder at the end of the table.

The video is of us... the previous night... at the arena. It's a very rough video, and was probably shot with a cell phone. But there, in the middle of the image, is Emma, jumping up and down and belting out *Crazy Road*, as if it's just another day at the office. The image is interrupted, after a couple seconds, by a local TV reporter...

> "Yes, music fans, the rumors are true. Last night, what many in the music world thought impossible, did actually happen. During a show at Moby Arena, for the first time since losing their bass player in the middle of a performance in Berlin..."

Someone changes the channel on the plasma TV at the end of the restaurant, and everyone – including us – turns their attention to it.

> "...the five original members of music sensation Audio Distortion not only turned up on stage together, but even took the time to play their first hit, Crazy Road, for over 5000 screaming fans, who had no idea what was going on. Armed with a notebook full of questions, this reporter has tried to find even one of the band members, most of whom have family in the local are, to no avail. So, to the members of Audio Distortion we send this message – tell us guys, tell your fans – are you back?"

"Oh jezzz..." Willie mutters.

"No kidding..." I add.

"Thanks, Janet," Stan says, handing her the tablet.

The look in her eyes tells us that she too, wants to know... she wants an answer to the question the TV reporter asked. Cadi gives her the only answer we have.

"We don't know, Janet... honest. At this point, we have to wait and see..."

She smiles, then turns and walks off. Seconds later, our waitress walks up, with the manager behind her.

"Hey guys! Ross," she says, pointing behind her, "says breakfast is on him."

"And..." Ross quickly adds, "you guys need to bail – fast. A friend of mine down at the Journal called and said word is out that you guys are here. Half the Denver, and all of the Ft. Collins press corps are about to swoop down on this place."

He looks right at Stan, tosses him a set of keys, and says, "Everyone knows Willie's BMW. Take my Explorer – it's in the back lot. I'll pick it up from your dad's house later."

Willie tosses him the keys to the X5, and says, "Just leave it at the Campbell's..."

"Crap!" I blurt out. "We've got to get to Emma's before they do. She'll freak..."

Twenty minutes later, we pull up behind Emma's house, and stop next to the gate. Stan produces the key, opens the gate, and once inside, we're astounded to find Emma sitting on the grass under the tree, strumming the acoustic guitar we gave her for her birthday, looking as if she's *expecting* us.

"I'm ready," she says, offering the guitar to me.

We stand staring at her, totally lost in the shock of the moment, none of us sure what to say or do.

"Emily... you did say when I was ready, right?"

"Emma... we have a problem..." I start to say, as I take the guitar.

"The press isn't a problem, unless *we* let them become one. Now come on, you guys owe me a song."

We glance at each other, then laugh – only because we don't know what else to do. We're worried about

Emma, and now it seems, she isn't worried about anything – not even the press.

Cadi sits down on the grass next to her, Stan on the other side of her, and Willie sits down facing them. I take a seat on the bricks around the tree, and on a beautiful summer morning, for only the third time in recorded history, *Audio Distortion* performs *We Are* – for an audience of one.

Jasper the cat.

twenty-three

freaked out

Emma Greene

The four of them follow me down the stairs to the basement, acting as if they expect to find something from one those horror movies at the bottom. It's actually rather comical.

When we reach the studio, I flip on the power and step aside. I'm right – they freak. But I force myself not to laugh.

"oh my god..." Cadi mumbles, which is quickly followed by "NO WAY!" from Stan, who goes right to the keyboard.

"The guitar goes over there, Emily," I say, pointing at an empty stand next to my other guitar.

Emily looks like a deer in headlights – pardon the pun – as she crosses the room and places the Ibanez in the stand. She looks at the mixing board mounted against the far wall, and it's as if she understands.

"This looks scarily familiar," she says.

"I was thinking the exact same thing," Willie adds, walking up behind her, and flipping the power switch.

"It should – it's a smaller version of the setup you guys have."

They both spin around at the same moment and look at me.

"Oh come on guys – I withdrew for a while. That doesn't make me crazy – which, according to a lot of what I read, is the general consensus," I say, smiling and taking a seat on a stool next to me. "When I heard what you two were up to, I called around and found out who was doing your work – which I should add, wasn't all that difficult. I told them I needed the same capabilities, but smaller."

They stand staring at me, while at the same time, Stan picks up Jasper and walks over to me.

"This," I add, waving my arms, "is what I got."

"Why?" Stan asks, putting Jasper in my lap.

This is when Cadi joins the conversation.

"She's been *writing*..."

First I hear pages being turned behind me, and know she's looking at the binder I left open on the desk. Then we hear the sound of a binder being slid out of the cabinet. Seconds later, after more page turning, I turn and look just in time to see her pull out a third binder and lay it on the desk between the others. I watch Willie, Emily, and Stan, join Cadi at the desk.

"Emma..." I hear Cadi say, in a totally disbelieving tone, *"are all of these full?"*

"Pretty close. A lot of it is just useless stuff... the confused, late night ramblings of a *'crazy'* teenager..."

They laugh, and roll their eyes.

"I had a lot of stuff I needed to get out of my head..." I pause, glance at Stanley, and smile, "And... out of my heart, too. But, I'm willing to bet that, between the five of us, we can find enough in there to make a record..."

One at a time, they straighten up, look first at each other – as if to be sure they heard what they think they did – and then turn to face me.

"*A record?*" Emily asks, just above a whisper.

"Yeah..." I reply, looking right at her, "if you guys can find the time and if, as Matt put it, 'you guys are up to it'..."

Instantly, big smiles cover every one of their faces, and the magic twinkle that fills their eyes every time we play together, returns. Just watching it makes my heart swell. Fighting the urge to cry, I turn and look at Cadi.

"How much of this can you *really* take? We *all* saw you using your inhaler onstage..."

Cadi smiles, steps over and first gives Jasper a good scratch behind the ears, then takes both my hands in hers.

"The studio stuff, I can handle. If the plan is to be onstage again regularly, I'll need time to get myself in shape. Playing in the orchestra is simple, no effort stuff. Last night reminded me of what it is *Audio Distortion* does. I won't try that again until I'm ready – until my doctor says I'm ready. In fact, it's my doctors who keep saying my daily activities are 'unrestricted'. Give me a month, and we'll test their theory."

I smile, and gently squeeze her hands.

"We *needed* last night, Emma – *all of us* – which is why I did it. You guys need to know what you're dealing with this time – which is why I broke out the inhaler. I mean, seriously – like we could perform *Crazy Road* without the 'slide'?"

Everyone laughs.

"And... *no matter what the situation*, Cadi, *you tell us* when you need to stop – right?" Stan quickly asks.

"*Absolutely!*" Cadi replies.

Then Emily, who's been quietly turning pages in one of the binders, straightens up and faces me.

"So… are we a band again?" she asks, so softly we barely hear her.

I let go of Cadi's hands, hand Jasper to her, slide off the stool, take Emily's hands, and watch her eyes glass over and the tears build in them.

"Emily… we never *stopped* being a band. I just needed some time to dwell on the fact that the five of us have always been *far more than just a band*…"

In seconds, she and I are crying like fools…

twenty-four

creating

Emma Greene

It takes the four of them three days to sift through all the binders in my basement – at one point, they have at least half of them lying open, covering pretty much the entire room. Eventually they come up with twelve songs they want to record right away, and nine others they want to 'work on'.

I find it interesting and maybe even a bit amusing that, although Emily and Willie have a state-of-the-art studio, less than three hours away by air, they choose to work in my basement. Stan – with the help of some of the kids from school – 'borrows' some instruments, and after eleven weeks, of fourteen hour days, I have to admit that, between the five of us, we do manage to create what sound like *Audio Distortion* songs.

Seeing the intensity the four of them exhibit, as we create *Audio Distortion*'s second record, makes me feel just a bit guilty. I know it's me – and my problems – that took this away from them. But now, that's over.

Fate and destiny have taken as much from me as they can, and I now realize that *the band* – not my 'gifts' – is the trade-off.

These four special people will, for the extended future, be my life and family.

At dinner one evening, we listen as Stan's dad explains what's going to happen when we tell the record company we're ready to go back to work. Fortunately for us, his construction and investing background makes Mr. Campbell an excellent advisor in things like contracts.

Anyhow, although – thanks again to Mr. Campbell – we as a group, own the name *Audio Distortion*, if we ever record under the name again, the record company gets dibs on the first two records. Heck, considering we pretty much self-destructed in the middle of a tour they financed, we figure we owe them *at least* that much.

Even though Mr. Campbell urges us – based on our contract – to tell the record company what we plan to do, before we tell anyone else, we have a different idea. Instead of 'following protocol' and 'asking permission' before talking to the press, we send the demo we made in my basement, directly to the company's production manager in a plain brown envelope, with a handwritten note that says, *'yeah... we're back'* with five signatures under it.

Kids... what are ya gonna do?

twenty-five

completion

Emma Greene

Thirteen weeks to the day after she spilled her – or actually *our* – guts on her show, Emily calls Donna Dollar. Again. This time, from my kitchen.

"Can I borrow your show again, Donna?"

"What do you mean, 'borrow my show'?"

"Say yes, and you'll find out," Emily replies, as the rest of us laugh.

"When?"

"When is the soonest you can do a live show?"

"Probably Friday. We have a taped two-parter that has to run back-to-back and a previously scheduled live show on Thursday. We can reschedule Friday's taped show, and go live. Is that the plan?"

"Only if you say it is. It is *your* show…"

"Emily… I have a very weird feeling about this."

"Good, so it's a date?"

"Like I would say 'no'? I'll set it up. Where are you going to be staying? We'll send a car for you."

"Don't bother. We'll get to the studio on our own."

"*We?*"

"Yeah… we. *Audio Distortion*. See you then."

Emily disconnects the call before Donna can reply, which cracks all of us up.

"This is going to be too cool," Willie offers.

Stan, who's reading a text message, looks up from his phone and says, "The promoter sent you a counter offer, Emma. They'll reschedule the six cancelled shows, make them open seating, but at $18 a ticket – instead of the $15 you asked for – until each venue is sold out. They want to work with us, but say they have to at least break even. They mentioned that if we manage to pull off multiple shows at even one location, we might make..."

"Not important," Emily blurts out, right in the middle of Stan's sentence. "What *is* important is that we clean up our reputation."

Everyone nods their agreement.

"In return..." Stan continues, standing up and walking over next to me, stopping and holding his phone where I can read the screen.

"We agree to use them to promote our next tour, assuming there is going to be one," I finish, glancing at Stanley, then looking at the rest of them.

"Seems more than fair," Cadi offers.

"You certain you're up to this, Cadi?" I ask, turning to look at her.

"As long as it isn't six shows in six nights, I can do it," she instantly replies.

"Well then, it looks like *Audio Distortion* is going to *finish* its first world tour after all," I say, smiling at all of them. "Willie, call Richard and tell him to load the equipment – we're back in business."

I stick out my hands, and after two years, the five *original* members of *Audio Distortion*, do their secret backstage handshake.

And, of course, we break up laughing.

twenty-six

the return

Emily Tao

Donna's show does what we intend – lets the world know we're ready to try again.

The same day I called Donna, the promoter and our record company leaked word that, not only are we back together, but we intend to make good on the cancelled shows. At Donna's show, five days later, we discover that four of the six venues have requested second shows.

Like I told Donna during our last interview, *Audio Distortion fans are the best!*

We end up taking a number of on-air calls from fans, most of them wanting to know when, and if, we'll be recording new songs.

The answer to that is simple. Once Richard listened to the demo we sent him, he pretty much freaked out, and immediately scheduled studio time for us to record the masters. Based on his time schedule, in about four months – the amount of time we expect it will take us to do the rescheduled shows – the record company will be releasing our first new single, for digital download. And, based solely on Emma's staunch, and unwavering insistence, they even agree to make it FREE!

Before we leave, and without any warning to Donna, we offer to perform *Replay* – the song that will be released first – for the studio audience. Their response amazes all of us.

All in all, it turns into an awesome day, and seeing Emma and Cadi, back to being themselves, makes it that much better.

Audio Distortion is indeed, back.

twenty-seven

replay

Emma Greene

"*Hey Emma! Whacha doin'?*" Georgie asks, as she races across my kitchen, sliding to a stop next to me. Seconds later, Stanley comes in behind her.

"Checking Billboard to see where our CD is this week."

She steps up to the table, and slowly runs her finger down the monitor of my laptop, stopping when she reaches the number '3' on the left side of the list – which is next to the title *'Audio Distortion – Replay'*.

"Number *three?* Oh come on! What do *they* know?" she blurts out, making Stanley and me laugh.

"Well, not as much as you apparently," Stanley offers, poking her gently in the ribs.

"Well... over at my school, *Audio Distortion* is NUMBER ONE!" she yells, spinning around and first hugging her brother, then hugging me.

So fans, you up for a world tour?
*Just reach over and hit '**REPLAY**'*

This story is actually just getting started.

Watch for

Journeys End

The next chapter in the lives of Emma, Stanley, Emily, Willie, and Cadi.

The phenomenon the world is calling

Audio Distortion

Available in print and digital formats online

amazon.com

Audio-Distortion.com

createspace.com/4334672